PENGUIN CLASSICS

THE SORROWS OF YOUNG WERTHER

JOHANN WOLFGANG VON GOETHE was born in Frankfurt-on-Main in 1749. He studied at Leipzig, where he showed interest in the occult, and at Strassburg, where Herder introduced him to Shakespeare's works and to folk poetry. He produced some essays and lyrical verse, and at twenty-two wrote *Götz von Berlichingen*, a play which brought him national fame and established him in the current *Sturm und Drang* movement. This was followed by the novel *The Sorrows of Young Werther* in 1774, which was an even greater success.

Goethe began work on *Faust*, and *Egmont*, another tragedy, before being invited to join the government of Weimar. His interest in the classical world led him to leave suddenly for Italy in 1786 and the *Italian Journey* recounts his travels there. *Iphigenia in Tauris* and *Torquato Tasso*, classical dramas, were written at this time. Returning to Weimar, Goethe started the second part of *Faust*, encouraged by Schiller. In 1806 he married Christiane Vulpius. During this late period he finished his series of *Wilhelm Meister* books and wrote many other works, including *The Oriental Divan* (1819). He also directed the State Theatre and worked on scientific theories in evolutionary botany, anatomy and colour. Goethe completed *Faust* in 1832, just before he died.

MICHAEL HULSE studied at the University of St Andrews, and since 1977 has taught at the Universities of Erlangen, Eichstätt and Cologne in Germany. Among his translations are Luise Rinser's *Prison Journal* (Penguin 1989), Jakob Wassermann's *Caspar Hauser* (Penguin Classics 1992) and fiction by Botho Strauss and Elfriede Jelinek. An award-winning poet, his most recent collection is *Eating Strawberries in the Necropolis* (1991).

JOHANN WOLFGANG VON GOETHE

THE SORROWS OF
YOUNG WERTHER

Translated with an Introduction and Notes
by Michael Hulse

PENGUIN BOOKS

PENGUIN BOOKS

Published by the Penguin Group
Penguin Books Ltd, 27 Wrights Lane, London W8 5TZ, England
Penguin Books USA Inc., 375 Hudson Street, New York, New York 10014, USA
Penguin Books Australia Ltd, Ringwood, Victoria, Australia
Penguin Books Canada Ltd, 10 Alcorn Avenue, Toronto, Ontario, Canada M4V 3B2
Penguin Books (NZ) Ltd, 182–190 Wairau Road, Auckland 10, New Zealand

Penguin Books Ltd, Registered Offices: Harmondsworth, Middlesex, England

Die Lieden des jungen Werthers first published 1774
This translation published in Penguin Classics 1989
9 10 8

Printed in England by Clays Ltd, St Ives plc
Set in Linotype 10 on 12 pt Ehrhardt

❧ *INTRODUCTION* ❧

I

'This spring,' wrote Christian Kestner in 1772, 'a certain Goethe came here. He is from Frankfurt, apparently a Doctor of Law, twenty-three years old, and the only son of a very wealthy father. He has come at his father's wish to look for a practice, but he himself inclines more to perusal of Homer, Pindar, etc., and whatever else his genius, his way of thinking and his heart move him to.'

The small town of Wetzlar, forty miles north of Frankfurt, then had a population of about 4,000, nearly a quarter of whom were employed at court. When Goethe registered at the *Reichskammergericht* on 25 May, his chances of following both his father and his grandfather in acquiring valuable experience and contacts in Wetzlar must have been excellent. But Goethe, already the author of striking poems as well as *Götz von Berlichingen* and other early dramatic works, was more likely to be found lying in the grass beneath a tree, philosophizing with his friends Gotter, von Goué, von Kielmansegge and König, than applying himself to a career. Alone or in company, Goethe would walk to the nearby village of Garbenheim, read his Homer or Goldsmith or the Bible, talk to the villagers and the children and sit in the shade of the linden trees. A schoolmaster's daughter who outlived the writer, dying two years after him in 1834, never forgot either Goethe or the other young gentleman, Jerusalem, and would show visitors to the village a wooden seat (the *Wertherstuhl*) which Goethe had sat on.

Not long after his arrival in Wetzlar, Goethe was at a ball in nearby Volpertshausen, and for the first time met a young woman called Charlotte Buff. In the same letter to his friend August von Hennings, Christian Kestner recorded the circumstances: 'On 9 June 1772 it happened that Goethe was at the same ball in the country as my girl

5

and I. I was unable to be there from the start, and followed on horse, so my girl drove out with other companions. Dr Goethe was one of those in the carriage, and that was where he first became acquainted with Lottchen. [. . .] He did not know that she was no longer free. [. . .] Lottchen made a complete conquest.'

Charlotte Buff, than aged nineteen, was the second eldest of the eleven children of Heinrich Adam Buff, the *Deutschorden*'s resident officer in Wetzlar and a widower. An attractive blue-eyed blonde, Charlotte was a natural, witty and spirited girl. Christian Kestner first met her when she was fifteen and was impressed, finding her unforced, kindly and polite in manner, not only contented within herself but also the cause of happiness in others. During the next few years, Kestner's affection and respect increased, especially following the mother's death in 1771, when Lotte assumed a position of authority and responsibility within the family, doing so with an ease and warmth of heart that made her both indispensable and dearly loved. Lotte returned Kestner's love, and at the time of Goethe's four-month stay in Wetzlar it was widely known that Kestner was Lotte's 'intended': that was the word by which Goethe and his friends referred to him and, forty years later, writing his autobiographical *Dichtung und Wahrheit*, Goethe again used the word rather than name Kestner.

With four decades of hindsight, Goethe recorded that he found Lotte pleasing and cheerful, pure and healthy, and noted that 'wherever she was, an atmosphere of lighthearted serenity prevailed'. Not least because she gave promise of domestic bliss, he thought her a young woman any man would want to call his own. Interestingly, he also described Lotte as a woman more likely to inspire contentment than violent passions. He took a liking to Christian Kestner, who was notable for his 'calm and even behaviour, clarity of opinions, and firmness in action and speech'. Goethe found Kestner diligent and sensible.

Christian Kestner, for his part, plainly thought Goethe an exceptional young man. 'He has a great many talents, is a true genius and a man of character, and has an extraordinarily vivid imagination, which leads him to express himself mostly in images and parables,' he wrote to von Hennings. 'He is altogether a man of violent emotion, yet he often has considerable self-control. The cast of his mind is noble, and he is free enough of prejudice to behave as he sees fit without troubling whether it is to the taste of the rest, or fashionable, or permitted by prevailing attitudes. He loathes all kinds of compulsion. He loves children and can keep himself well occupied with them.'

Between Lotte and Goethe and Kestner a friendship developed, a friendship that transformed the delightful summer of 1772 into what the autobiographer retrospectively described as 'a genuine German idyll'. In *Dichtung und Wahrheit*, the ageing Goethe presented that long summer as a dreamily joyful season in which the beauty of the countryside provided the prose and the pure delights of affection the matching poesy. On rambles in fields and gardens, amid the ripening corn, hearing the lark, the three friends were inseparable. Or, at least, two of them were inseparable. There were times when 'the intended' was prevented by his business from taking further time off. At such times, Goethe and Lotte would go walking together.

Kestner was a man of sense and tolerance, and his instincts prompted him to friendship rather than unfounded jealousy, but nevertheless he was not altogether pleased with the closeness of Lotte and Goethe. As early as the end of June, he wrote in his diary: 'Afterwards, once my work was done, I went to see my girl, and found Dr Goethe there. [. . .] He loves her, and, however much of a philosopher he is, and however well-disposed he may be towards me, he does not care to see me coming to pass my time in pleasures with my girl. And I, though I too am well-disposed towards him, do not like to find him alone with my girl, entertaining her.'

In his autobiography, Goethe implied that the new three-way friendship was free of friction, and suggested that whatever pain and frustration he had felt in Lotte's company was a natural part of that happiness we experience when we desire what we cannot have. 'If, as they say, the greatest happiness is to be found in longing,' he wrote, 'and if true longing must always be directed to something unattainable, then everything conspired,' he continued, referring to himself in the third person, 'to make the youth whose fortunes we are following the happiest mortal on earth. His affection for a woman who was already promised to someone else, his efforts to make masterpieces of foreign literature a part of our own, and his own, and his endeavours to capture Nature not only in words but also with a pencil and brush, albeit without any proper technique: any of these

7

would have been sufficient to swell his heart and weigh upon his breast.'

That both Goethe and Lotte behaved within the limits imposed by natural integrity and innocent friendship is unquestioned. That this was possible without any strain seems very unlikely, partly because of the relief Goethe experienced when he had written the novel and exorcized the past, and partly because the moment came during the summer of 1772 when Lotte was obliged to tell Goethe plainly that he must not expect her to return his love. 'She told him that he should not hope for anything but friendship,' wrote Kestner in his diary on 16 August. 'He was pale and very downcast.'

Less than a month later, Goethe was gone. On 10 September he spent the evening with Lotte and Kestner, and their talk, at Lotte's prompting, turned to life after death, and whether there could be a reunion after the departure. Once again, Goethe was dejected. At seven o'clock the next morning he quit Wetzlar without warning. A farewell note addressed to Lotte looked forward to a future meeting, dwelt on the sweet sorrow of their final evening, and added: 'I am alone now, and may shed my tears. I leave you both to your happiness, and will not be gone from your hearts.'

Lotte (Kestner's diary tells us) had tears in her eyes when she read Goethe's note, while Kestner was obliged to defend Goethe against the accusation of rude abruptness. Meanwhile, the young writer himself was making his way to Koblenz, where he met his friend Merck, the authoress Sophie von La Roche and her privy councillor husband, and their sixteen-year-old eldest daughter Maximiliane. 'It is very pleasant,' Goethe tells us in *Dichtung und Wahrheit*, 'if a new passion awakens within us before the old one has quite faded away.' Goethe liked Maximiliane immensely, and Lotte in the novel resembles Maximiliane von La Roche more closely in physical appearance than she does Charlotte Buff. With Maximiliane, however, Goethe was again destined for disappointment, and two years later she married a middle-aged Frankfurt merchant.

Goethe remained in close letter contact with his Wetzlar friends, and was disturbed at the beginning of October to hear a rumour (which proved unfounded) that his friend von Goué had committed suicide. 'I honour the deed,' wrote Goethe to Kestner on 10 October, though he added: 'I hope I shall never trouble my friends with news of

8

such a kind.' Not three weeks later a second suicide was reported, and this time the report was correct: on the night of 29 October, Karl Wilhelm Jerusalem shot himself. He died around midday on the 30th and was buried the same evening.

Slightly Goethe's senior, Jerusalem was born into a strongly religious family in March 1747 in Wolfenbüttel, went to college in Braunschweig (Brunswick) and afterwards studied law in Leipzig at the same time as Goethe, and then in Göttingen, where he graduated in 1770. Thought an agreeable and sound young man, he had the respect of one of the pre-eminent writers of the time, Lessing. In September 1771 he took a job in Wetzlar as secretary to von Hoefler, the ambassador of Braunschweig. In Wetzlar he busied himself with painting, poetry and philosophy in his free time, and was occasionally one of the number when Goethe and his friends met in Wetzlar or Garbenheim, though he and Goethe were never close. Jerusalem apparently did not share Christian Kestner's high opinion of Goethe, describing him in somewhat superior tones, in a letter of July 1772, as a 'fop' and a 'scribbler'.

In *Dichtung und Wahrheit*, Goethe remembered Jerusalem as a polite, round-faced, gentle, blue-eyed, fair-haired youth. 'He wore the clothes that were usual, in imitation of the English, in northern Germany: a blue frock-coat, a buff leather waistcoat and breeches.' Goethe particularly recalled Jerusalem's taste for drawings of deserted landscapes, and his passion for another man's wife. Christian Kestner, recording that Jerusalem had already been cold-shouldered by Wetzlar's high society, that he was of a solitary and brooding disposition and given to taking long lonely walks by moon-light, and that he had penned an essay in defence of suicide, felt that that passion for Elisabeth Herd had finally broken Jerusalem. 'I do not believe she cares for gallant amours, and in any case her husband is extremely jealous; so his love finally put paid to his heart's ease and peace of mind.'

On hearing the news at the beginning of November, Goethe immediately wrote to Kestner: 'The poor fellow! I remember return-ing from a walk and meeting him in the moonlight, and saying to myself: he is in love. It was loneliness, God knows, that ate away at his heart.—I have known him for seven years, though I talked to him seldom; when I left I took one of his books with me, and I shall keep it now and remember him as long as I live.' Goethe was in Wetzlar from 6 to 11 November, and took the opportunity to find out the details of Jerusalem's death. Later that month he also received a meticulous written account which he had asked Kestner for, and on which he was to base the final pages of his novel in due course. Once in possession of the precise facts, Goethe (according to *Dichtung und Wahrheit*) beheld the structure of the novel in its entirety.

Christian Kestner's account reported a story that was circulating in Wetzlar, to the effect that Jerusalem had declared his love to Elisabeth Herd. Frau Herd, keeping the young man at arm's length, had told her husband of the scene, asking him to forbid Jerusalem access to their house, which her husband did. At this point Jerusalem sent a note to Kestner, asking for a loan of his pistols for a journey he intended to make, and Kestner, ignorant of what might be in Jerusalem's mind, complied with the request.

Jerusalem spent the afternoon sorting his papers, paying debts and walking. That evening he had the fire made up and had his servant bring him a jug of wine. He told the servant he would be making an early start in the morning, and the servant accordingly went to bed without undressing, in order to be ready when needed. Jerusalem then wrote two letters, one to his family and a second to Herd, apologizing for disturbing the peace of his home. Kestner speculated that Jerusalem might have written a third letter, to von Hoefler, and suggested the ambassador might be suppressing it in order to make Jerusalem's disappointment in love appear the major cause of the tragedy. The ambassador had been dissatisfied with Jerusalem and had wanted him replaced, and may have felt responsible on this account.

Between midnight and one, Jerusalem shot himself. A Franciscan monk heard the shot and saw the flash of the powder; but, since everything remained quiet, he thought no more about it. Jerusalem appeared to have killed himself sitting at his desk, Kestner reported. 'The back-rest of the chair was bloody, so were the arm-rests. He sank down from the chair. There was a great deal of blood on the floor. He must have thrashed about on the floor in his blood [. . .] and then dragged himself to the window. [. . .] (He was fully clothed, wearing his boots and his blue coat and buff waistcoat.)'

The servant entered at six the next morning and found his master still alive but unable to do anything but groan. A doctor was summoned and 'to crown it all he opened a vein in his arm'. The news reached Kestner and, thinking with horror of his pistols, he hurried to Jerusalem's rooms. 'His lungs still produced a fearful death-rattle, one moment feebly, the next louder; his end was expected soon. He had drunk only a single glass of the wine. [. . .] *Emilia Galotti* lay open on a desk by the window.'

Jerusalem died around midday, and was buried the same night shortly before eleven. Kestner reported that barbers' apprentices bore him to the grave, and that a cross was carried ahead of Jerusalem. He added the plain statement which Goethe subsequently chose to use as the final words of his novel: 'No priest attended him.'

Kestner and Lotte married in April 1773, and let Goethe know after the event. Maximiliane von La Roche married in January 1774. Then Goethe began to write.

II

It can come as no great surprise that *Die Leiden des jungen Werthers*, published by Weygand in Leipzig later in 1774, was received in its time (and continues to be read) as partly autobiographical, partly biographical. Writing to von Hennings in November 1774, Kestner noted plainly that in the first part of the novel Werther was Goethe, and in the second Jerusalem. Goethe himself, later describing the writing of the work as the business of four weeks, during which time he proceeded with the unconscious certainty of a sleepwalker, wrote in *Dichtung und Wahrheit* of the sense of freedom and deliverance he experienced after his labours, and specifically spoke of a 'confession'. And indeed, in a real sense *Werther* is the first great achievement of what a later age was to label 'confessional' literature.

There were naïve readers, though, who were not content for Goethe to transform 'reality into poesy': the knowledge that real events lay behind Goethe's fiction was taken as an excuse for maudlin indulgences. In spring 1776 a torchlit procession made its way to Jerusalem's grave, where a popular Werther poem by C. E. von

Reitzenstein was sung, speeches made and flowers left. Pilgrims came from all over Europe. John Murray's *Handbook for Travellers on the Continent* told the nineteenth-century English traveller where to find Jerusalem's grave, Charlotte's fountain and the linden tree Goethe liked to sit beneath. At Garbenheim, an innkeeper heaped up a mound of earth and would solemnly tell visitors that it was Werther's [*sic*] grave. One group of five English pilgrims toasted Werther over this grave, emptied the rest of the bottle on the earth and then, daggers drawn, declaimed speeches before making gifts to the villagers. Knowing that there was once a reality which had been fictionalized into a different realm of experience was not enough: 'reality' had to include the 'poesy', and was sanctified by it.

Tales of a far more maudlin indulgence have been greatly exaggerated. An essential part of the Werther legend has always insisted that there was a spate of '*Liebestod* all over Europe', in the words of a recent poem by Michael Hofmann. But there seems little evidence that Goethe's novel prompted a suicide epidemic. A woman named Fanni von Ickstatt jumped to her death from a tower of the Frauenkirche in Munich, but whether the poem which promptly appeared, blaming the tragedy on Goethe's novel, was right to do so cannot be decided. More strikingly, another young woman drowned herself in the River Ilm behind Goethe's garden in Weimar, in January 1778. Christine von Lassberg had been deserted by her lover, and went to her death with a copy of *Werther* in her pocket. Whether she would have killed herself if Goethe's novel had not influenced her is a moot point. At all events, the young men of Europe contented themselves with dressing in blue frock-coats and buff waistcoats, and sensibly preferred not to pull the trigger. When James Hackman murdered Martha Reay outside Covent Garden in 1779, and then tried to shoot himself (but failed), Sir Herbert Croft worked up the affair into an epistolary novel titled *Love and Madness*, which supposed Hackman to have been influenced by *Werther* and even to have written a set of 'Lines found, after Werter's death, upon the ground by the pistol'; but whether the real James Hackman had indeed read *Werther* is doubtful, and why it should prompt him to murder seems even more doubtful. The Hackman case was later made the subject of a further novel, *Der englische Werther*, published by Wilhelm Häring in 1843 under the pseudonym Willibald Alexis.

12

Whether the myth of a suicide epidemic has any truth to it or not, many of Goethe's contemporaries were ready to assume that the novel might exert a corrupting influence, and a heated debate raged over the question. One of the pre-eminent writers of the time, Wieland, reviewed Goethe's novel in the *Teutsche Merkur* in December 1774, and observed that to invite the reader's pity for one suicide, and to show that a soft heart and a fiery imagination could be destructive, was far from writing a defence of suicide in general. The Leipzig censors thought otherwise. When the Leipzig theological faculty applied for a ban on the novel, on the grounds that it recommended suicide, the city council imposed the ban within two days. In Denmark too a proposed translation was prohibited. Nicolai, who wrote a parodic alternative ending for the novel, disliked the apparent defence of suicide, while the dramatist Lenz, in an un-published commentary on the morality of *Werther*, noted that to see the novel thus was like interpreting Homer's *Iliad* as an incitement to anger, discord and enmity. In a letter of May 1775, Lichtenberg dryly remarked: 'the smell of a pancake is a more powerful reason for remaining in this world than all young Werther's supposedly lofty conclusions are for quitting it.' Lichtenberg imagined two illustra-tions, before and after, the first showing an unhappy lover clutching a pistol and a knife, the novel and a pancake on the table before him, and beneath the picture the words, 'My bane, my antidote are both before me' (from Addison's *Cato*), and the second showing the pistol unheeded, the knife in the pancake, half the pancake in the young man's mouth, and underneath the picture Caesar's words: *'Jacta est alea.'* Goethe himself felt sufficiently affected by the debate to add a quatrain motto to each part of the novel in the 1775 reprint; the motto for the second part ends with the injunction to be a man and not follow Werther.

Imitating Werther's life and death was one thing, and imitating the book in which he appeared was another. The success of *Werther* was rapid and immense. The novel was soon translated into every major European language. There were poems about Werther. There were plays about Werther. There were operas about Werther. At the Prater in Vienna there was a Werther fireworks display. In Fleet Street in London, Mrs Salmon's Royal Historical Wax-Work showed 'the much-admired Group of The Death of Werter, attended by Charlotte and her Family'. Werther songs were sung. Meissen porcelain showed Werther scenes. Ladies wore Werther jewellery and their scent was Eau de Werther. They carried Werther fans and wore Werther gloves. By 1799, Werther had gone round the world and was returning to Germany from the Far East: an enterprising Chinese, noticing the popularity of the character, had begun producing Werther paintings in the Chinese style and sending them to Europe.

The fifteen years following first publication were the heyday of *Werther* fever. A French translation appeared in 1776, and *The Sorrows of Werter: A German Story*, in a translation by Daniel Malthus (father of the economist), in 1779. Those were lean years for English literature. Fielding and Richardson, Sterne and Smollett, Goldsmith and Gray were all dead, and for a few years Goethe's novel dominated the English scene. Influenced by Richardson's epistolary novels and Goldsmith's *The Vicar of Wakefield*, Young and Gray, *Hamlet* and 'Ossian', it offered a familiar elegiac atmosphere, and scenes involving children, patriarchal country life and wild, tempestuous landscape, such as the prevailing English taste could readily accept. Quickly assimilated, though read only as a sentimentally tragic love story, *Werther* provided a talking point: Fanny Burney recorded being asked her opinion of the novel by Queen Charlotte, who disliked it, and at the Spring Garden Coffee House in London there was a meeting to debate whether Charlotte was justified in accepting Werther's visits after her marriage to Albert. Werther and Charlotte appeared in countless poems, and this sonnet by Charlotte Smith, by no means one of the worst, suggests the qualities Goethe's novel was felt to represent and the responses it appealed to:

> Make there my tomb; beneath the lime-trees shade,
>   Where grass and flowers in wild luxuriance wave;
> Let no memorial mark where I am laid,
>   Or point to common eyes the lover's grave!
> But oft at twilight morn, or closing day,
>   The faithful friend, with fault'ring step shall glide,
> Tributes of fond regret by stealth to pay,
>   And sigh o'er the unhappy suicide.
> And sometimes, when the Sun with parting rays

Gilds the long grass that hides my silent bed,
The tears shall tremble in my CHARLOTTE's eyes;
   Dear, precious drops!—they shall embalm the dead;
Yes! CHARLOTTE o'er the mournful spot shall weep,
Where her poor WERTER—and his sorrows sleep.

It is interesting that the scene that clinches this sonnet does not appear in the novel: there is a firmness in Goethe's treatment of his material which went unappreciated by his more sentimental contemporaries. Charlotte weeping over Werther's grave was a favourite scene amongst illustrators, and in Crabbe's 'The Parish Register' we read:

Fair prints along the paper'd wall are spread;
There, Werter sees the sportive children fed,
And Charlotte, here, bewails her lover dead.

By the time Crabbe wrote these lines in 1807, though, the English popularity of *Werther* was past its peak. Gone were the days when a few lines in the first letter could prompt the anonymous novel *Eleonora* (1785), or William James, in corrective vein, could write *The Letters of Charlotte during her Connexion with Werter* (1786), or the popular Mrs Kennedy could sing Werther songs at Vauxhall Gardens. After the French Revolution Goethe and Schiller and other German writers were identified with Jacobinism, and patriotic conservatives condemned them. Frederick Reynolds's play *Werter: a Tragedy* continued to be performed occasionally, but earnest Wertherism was supplanted in due course by the less fatalistic Romantic energy of Byronism, and by 1835 Longfellow could write: 'In England and America the book is sneered at. I think it is not understood.' Twenty years later, Goethe's English biographer Lewes baldly stated: '*Werther* is not much read nowadays, especially in England.'

Elsewhere in Europe, *Werther* became more firmly established. A French dramatic version, *Les Malheurs de l'Amour*, was printed at Berne in 1775, before the French translation of the novel appeared. The French could see that not only their favourite English writers but also Rousseau were behind Goethe's work: the Rousseau of *La Nouvelle Héloïse*, the Rousseau who in the first sentence of *Emile*

15

declared that the world was good as it left the hands of its Creator but bad once Man had been at work on it. Werther novels and poems and plays proliferated in France. La Rivière's *Werther, ou Le Délire de l'amour* held the stage for several years. Novels appeared in which the characters were French (*Le Nouveau Werther*, 1786) or the hero a heroine (*Werthérie*, 1791). Napoleon took Goethe's novel with him on his Egyptian campaign in 1798, and when he met the author in 1808 he told him he had read the book seven times. In late 1809 Goethe received a package from a far corner of the French-speaking world, Mauritius, and on opening it found *Sydner, ou les Dangers de l'imagination*, an imitation that had been published there in 1803.

Meanwhile, Holland had its own alexandrine Werther tragedy in 1786, and Italy a play by Sografi in 1794, which was performed in the open in the Roman amphitheatre at Verona and had quaint offshoots in a puppet play given in Naples and a tragicomic opera, *Carlotta e Werter* (1814), by Coccia. Lamartine, Mickiewicz and Gautier were among the admirers of Goethe's novel. In Gogol's *Dead Souls* (1842) the drunken Chichikov recited the Russian translation of a French Werther poem. The 1880s saw Dicenta's Spanish play *El suicidio de Werther* (1888) and Massenet's opera, first performed in Vienna in 1892. In 1894 the first Japanese translation was made. In 1903 Sarah Bernhardt was seen in a French stage version, prompting one critic to exclaim, 'hélas!' and, 'oof!' The uses to which Goethe's material have been put have not always been happy.

In Germany, Werther fever was so high that on 6 March 1775 Goethe was already writing to a friend: 'I am heartily tired of having poor Werther exhumed and dissected.' In Germany there were poems, songs and plays, and parodies too. Nicolai's *Freuden des jungen Werthers* told of the joys that could have been Werther's in place of his sorrows, and proposed an alternative ending. Albert, realizing Werther's intention, loads his pistols with pellets of chicken blood. Finding his friend in a pool of blood, he is able to explain to the would-be suicide that he is willing to relinquish his claim on Lotte. Werther leaps happily to his feet, exclaiming, 'Oh joy, oh bliss!' He marries Lotte, and they live in a contentment which is marred only by those usual domestic crises which (Nicolai implies) it is the task of the mature and responsible adult to cope with. An ex-traveller with grand ideas lays out an exotic oriental garden on the slope above Werther's modest retreat, and one day a flood from the waterfall above devastates Werther and Lotte's summerhouse. 'A genius makes a poor neighbour,' concludes Werther, by now thoroughly assimilated to that small world of bourgeois domesticity his prototype so yearned to be free of.

Nicolai's squib was sometimes reviewed (and even bound) together with Goethe's novel. It is a crude broadside which, though sympathetic to the compelling force of the original, still manages to miss Goethe's insistence on Werther's fatal and tragic flaw, but none the less the parody has valid points to make. The proto-Romantic cult of the genius exempt from the customary rules and judgements of society was characteristic of German writing of the *Sturm und Drang*, and once it was coupled with that sentimental, melancholy sensitivity which was known as *Empfindsamkeit* it produced an intellectual and emotional mood in which everyone (as Goethe put it in *Dichtung und Wahrheit*) felt he could be the Prince of Denmark. Nicolai's point was simply that that kind of genius was anti-social. Obeying society's rules is the better path to human contentment. Goethe disliked Nicolai's parody, perhaps because he was aware that the conflict between individual and society was indeed unresolved in his novel, and in himself. It was not long before he would make a good career at court in Weimar, chafing a little and even escaping to Italy, dramatizing tensions similar to Werther's in his play *Torquato Tasso*, and biding by the rules until a time came, after the French Revolution, when he could write: 'Only Law can give us Freedom.' The parodoxical conflict remained active within him throughout his life. In *Werther* it was virulent.

A later German writer directed attention to another aspect of the novel, that part which had caused Goethe to be thought a Jacobin by English conservatives in the 1790s. Writing in 1828, Heine, who had little patience with Werther's tragic love story or with the question of suicide, declared that the passage that dealt with Werther's exclusion from aristocratic society would have been recognized as the heart of the book if it had been published then rather than in the 1770s. Naturally Heine was overstating the case. And Goethe, in his old age, would have been reluctant to agree with him, since whatever firebrand inclinations he might once have had were a part of his remote past. Goethe was never much of a revolutionary, never one to exclaim that it was bliss to be alive in that dawn, unless it was meant as an expression of individual exhilaration: the insult that is offered Werther at the count's gathering has an essential place in the development of the novel's action, and in confirming Werther's position as something of a rejected outsider, but is only implicitly a scene of political moment. Nevertheless, Heine was right to draw attention to an aspect of the novel that Goethe's immediate contemporaries had succeeded in overlooking. Beyond the struggles of one individual to assert his own larger sense of his place in Creation, beyond Werther's frustration at feeling trapped by society's trammelling rules, a very real and discontented sense of the gap between aristocratic high society and the common folk remains persistently and fretfully present in the novel.

In Germany, the sentimental reading of the novel as a tragic love story alone, a reading made possible by the dark and overdrawn tastes of the age of *Empfindsamkeit*, was gradually supplanted by a grasp of the novel's social and political dimension, its profound understanding of the place of man in his natural environment and, above all, its sensitive exploration of the psychopathology of a gifted but ill-adjusted young man. An age more subtly alert to the relationship of an author to his fictive characters became willing and able to set aside the obsession with the original events and assess the artistry in Goethe's treatment of them: the aptness of the letter form as an expression of one-sided and lonely communication, the deftness of Goethe's orchestration of motifs and moods and the skill with which the author interposes an ironic distance between the reader and Werther without forfeiting a claim on sympathy for the unfortunate. The development of a more mature reading of the novel in Germany was assisted by familiarity with Goethe's later works. Outside Germany, that very popularity which had hurried Goethe to early international fame ironically proved an obstacle to the reception of his later works. Sir Walter Scott's translation of *Götz von Berlichingen*, and a French selection of Goethe's poems published in 1825, informed the purchaser that they were by the author of *Werther*. Only gradually did the full fertility and scope of Goethe's achievement become evident to readers outside Germany. *Werther* is a signal accomplishment, the first great tragic novel, a work of exhilarating style and insight. Considered in an *oeuvre* that also includes *Faust*,

Wilhelm Meister, *Elective Affinities*, delightful travel writing and auto-biography, several plays, essays, scientific studies and some of the greatest poetry ever written, it is astonishing.

Werther has often been translated into English, but it seems that since the first fever of the 1780s it has not been very much read, and Longfellow's feeling that 'it is not understood' may still be true today. Partly this is because the Anglo-Saxon image of a stuffy Sage of Weimar prevents Goethe's early novel from being read on its own terms. When Joyce admitted Gouty to the European triumvirate alongside Daunty and Shopkeeper, he found the very word to express an Anglo-Saxon conception of Goethe which is based almost entirely on the writer's patrician old age, a conception which sees him as huffy and puffy and pompous. Nothing could be further from the truth; but it is important to clear away this prejudice before approaching the energetic and tragic novel Goethe wrote at the age of twenty-four. It is less easy to account for one-sided readings which in their way are as naïve as the sentimental readings of Goethe's contemporaries. When Peter Porter refers in a poem to 'the world's most famous novel of self-pity', or Christopher Ricks, writing on Keats, speaks of 'the enfeebling Werther-ish romanticism of love as a moping and will-less affectation', we realize that a species of wilful damage has been wrought during the reading, and Goethe's novel has emerged maimed and battered. To complain of Werther's self-pity or lack of will is like complaining of Hamlet's procrastination. The weaknesses in Werther's character are certainly there. They are there for a reason. They are there as an essential part of the portrait of a man ill-equipped to cope with his life. They are there as the fatal flaws in a character likeable, generous, creative, spontaneous, responsive and full of vitality. And as such they must be accepted as the necessary premisses in a persuasive tragedy, as necessary components in a consummate work of art.

For this translation I have used the text of Goethe's final revision of the novel, published in 1787, as given in Volume 6 of the *Hamburger Ausgabe* of Goethe's works, edited by Erich Trunz.

Michael Hulse
Cologne
February 1988

THE SORROWS OF
YOUNG WERTHER

I have diligently collected everything I have been able to discover concerning the story of poor Werther, and here present it to you in the knowledge that you will be grateful for it. You cannot deny your admiration and love for his spirit and character, nor your tears at his fate.

And you, good soul, who feel a compulsive longing such as his, draw consolation from his sorrows, and let this little book be your friend whenever through fate or through your own fault you can find no closer companion.

BOOK ONE

4 May 1771

How happy I am to be away! My dear friend, what a thing is the heart of Man! To leave you, whom I love so, from whom I was inseparable, and to be happy! I know that you will forgive me. Were not my other attachments hand-picked by Fate to beset a heart such as mine with fears? Poor Leonore![1] And yet I was innocent. Was it my fault that, while I was taking pleasure and amusement in the wilful charms of her sister, a passion was growing in that poor heart? And yet—am I wholly innocent? Did I not nurture her feelings? Did I not take delight in those utterly true expressions of her nature which so often made us laugh, though they were far from ridiculous? Did I not —Oh, what a creature is Man, that he may bewail himself! I promise, dear friend, I promise I shall improve, and will not keep on chewing over some morsel of misfortune doled out by Fate, as I always have done; I mean to enjoy the present moment, and what is past will be over and done with. Of course you are right, my friend, that the pains people endure would be less if only—God knows why they are made that way!—if only they did not put so much imaginative energy into recalling the memory of past misfortune, rather than bear an indifferent present with equanimity.

Will you be so good as to tell my mother I shall deal with her business as well as I can and will give her news of it very soon. I have spoken to my aunt,[2] and found her far from being the wicked female she is made out to be at home. She is a buxom, vigorous woman with the kindest of hearts. I explained my mother's complaints concerning the portion of the inheritance that was withheld from her; she told me her reasons and motives, and the conditions on which she would be prepared to hand over everything, more indeed than we have demanded—In short, I do not wish to write about it now, but tell my

25

mother it will all turn out well. And once again, dear friend, I have found while seeing to this little matter that misunderstandings and lethargy perhaps lead to more complications in the affairs of the world than trickery and wickedness. At least, the two latter are surely less common.

For the rest, I feel most contented here. Solitude is precious balm to my heart in these paradisic parts; and the abundance of this youthful season gives warmth to a heart that is oft atremble with horror. Every tree, every hedgerow is a posy of blossoms, and one could wish to be a cockchafer, floating in a sea of wonderful scents and finding all one's nourishment there.

The town itself is disagreeable, but on the other hand there is an inexpressible natural beauty all around. It was this that moved the late Count von M. to lay out a garden[3] on one of these hills, which slope against each other in the most delightful and various of ways and form the prettiest of valleys. The garden is a simple one, and the moment one enters it one feels that it was designed not by some scientific gardener but by a feeling heart intending to take pleasure here. I have already shed many a tear for the count, in the tumbledown little summerhouse that was his favourite spot and now is mine too. Soon I shall be master of the garden; in these few days the gardener has already become attached to me, and he will not have cause to regret it.

10 May

A wonderful serenity has taken possession of my entire soul, as these sweet spring mornings have, which I am enjoying with my whole heart. I am alone and rejoicing in my life in these parts, which were created for just such souls as mine. I am so happy, dear friend, so absorbed in this feeling of peaceful existence, that my art is suffering. I could not draw now, not a single line, and yet I have never been a greater painter than in these moments. When the vapours rise about me in this lovely valley, and the sun shines high on the surface of the impenetrable darkness of my forest, and only single rays steal into the inner sanctum, and I lie in the long grass by the tumbling brook, and lower down, close to the earth, I am alerted to the thousand various little grasses; when I sense the teeming of the little world among the stalks, the countless indescribable forms of the grubs and flies, closer to my heart, and feel the presence of the Almighty who created us in His image, the breath of the All-loving who bears us aloft in perpetual joy and holds us there; my friend! if it grows dusky then before my eyes, and the world about me and the heavens lie peaceful in my soul like a lover—then I am often filled with longing, and think: ah, if only you could express this, if only you could breathe onto the paper in all its fullness and warmth what is so alive in you, so that it would mirror your soul as your soul is the mirror of God in His infinity!—My friend—But it will be the end of me. The glory of these visions, their power and magnificence, will be my undoing.

12 May

I do not know whether treacherous spirits haunt these parts, or whether the warm, heavenly fantasy that makes everything seem like paradise is in my own heart. Right outside the town there is a spring,[4] a spring that holds me in thrall like Melusine[5] and her sisters.—You go down a little slope and come to a vault where some twenty steps descend to where the clearest of water pours forth from the marble rock. The low wall about the spring above, the tall trees that shade the place, the coolness of the spot, all of this has something both attractive and awesome. Not a day goes by but I spend an hour sitting there. And the girls come out from the town to fetch water,[6] that most innocent and necessary of tasks which in former times was done by the daughters of kings themselves. When I sit there the patriarchal ways come vividly to life about me, and I see them all, the ancestral fathers, making friends and courting by the spring, and I sense the benevolent spirits that watch over springs and wells. Oh, anyone who cannot share this feeling must never have refreshed himself at a cool spring after a hard day's summer walking.

27

13 May

You ask if you should send me my books?—My dear fellow, I implore you, for God's sake keep the things from me! I do not want to be led on, stimulated, inspired any more, for this heart of mine is turbulent enough of its own accord; what I need is soothing lullabies, and I have found them in abundance in my Homer.[7] How often do I lull my tumultuous blood to rest; for you have seen nothing as changeably unquiet as this heart. Dear friend! do I need to tell you that, you who have so often endured seeing me pass from sorrow to excessive joy, from sweet melancholy to destructive passion? And I am treating my poor heart like an ailing child; every whim is granted. Tell no one of this; there are people who would take it amiss.

15 May

The common people of the town already know and love me, the children in particular. Something sad has struck me. When at first I joined them and asked them friendly questions about this and that, some of them supposed I was out to mock them and gave me a distinctly uncouth reception. I did not let this trouble me unduly; yet I felt very strongly something that I have often noticed, that people of some standing always keep coldly aloof from the common folk, as if they believe they would lose if they approached them; and then there are irresponsible characters and nasty jokers who appear to condescend, but only to make the poor people feel their cockiness all the more.

I well know we are not equal, nor can be; but I maintain that he who supposes he must keep his distance from what they call the rabble, to preserve the respect due to him, is as much to blame as a coward who hides from his enemy for fear of being beaten.

Recently I went to the spring and came upon a young servant girl who had set down her pitcher on the bottom-most step and was looking round to see if some companion would come and help her lift it onto her head. I went down and looked at her.—'May I assist the young maid?' said I.—She blushed from top to toe.—'Oh no, sir!'

said she.—'No standing on ceremony,' said I.—She set her headgear[8] straight, and I helped her. She thanked me and climbed the steps.

17 May

I have made all manner of acquaintance but have yet to meet with any society. I do not know what it is that attracts people to me; so many like me and attach themselves to me, and then it hurts me to find that we are travelling the same stretch for only a short way. If you ask how the people are here I have to answer: just as they are everywhere! The human race is a monotonous affair. Most people spend the greatest part of their time working in order to live, and what little freedom remains so fills them with fear that they seek out any and every means to be rid of it. What a thing our human destiny is!

But the folk are of a very fine kind! When at times I forget myself and, together with them, enjoy the pleasures that are still available to mankind, such as sitting round a crowded table joking in innocent, open-hearted warmth, or taking a ride or dancing when one feels like it, or such things, it has a very good effect on me; but then I must be certain not to think of those many other powers lying dormant in me, mouldering in disuse, which I must needs keep carefully concealed. Ah, it trammels the whole heart so.—And still! to be misunderstood is my fate.

Ah, that the friend of my youth[9] is dead! Ah, that I ever knew her!—I might say: You are a fool! You are looking for something that cannot be found on earth! And yet she was mine. I felt that heart, that great soul, in whose presence I seemed to be more than I was, because I was all that I could be. Great God! Was there any single power in my soul that lay unused? Was I not able to reveal to her all of the wonderful feeling with which my heart embraces Nature? When we were together, were we not forever weaving the finest of sensibility and the keenest of wit, all of whose manifestations, even when they went too far, were marked with the stamp of genius? And now!—Ah, she was years older than me, and went to her grave before me. Never shall I forget her, never her firm understanding and her divine tolerance.

29

Some days ago I met a certain young V., an honest youth with most pleasing features. He has but recently left the academies, and, while he does not consider himself wise, he none the less believes he knows more than others do. He was hardworking too, as I could tell from a number of things; in short, his knowledge is quite presentable. Since he had heard that I draw a good deal and know Greek (two outlandish things in these parts), he approached me and hauled forth a great deal of learning, from Batteux to Wood, from de Piles to Winckelmann, and assured me he had read the first part of Sulzer's theory right through and possessed a manuscript by Heyne concerning the study of antiquity.[10] This was all fine by me.

There is another worthy man I have now got to know, the manager[11] of the royal estate, an open man of good heart. They say it brings joy to the spirit to see him among his children, nine of them; his eldest daughter in particular is highly spoken of. He has invited me to his home, and I mean to visit him in the very near future. He lives in a royal hunting lodge an hour and a half from here, where he was given permission to move after the death of his wife, as he found it too painful to remain here in town, in the official residence.

One or two other bizarre characters have crossed my path too, and everything about them is unbearable, and most intolerable of all are their protestations of friendship.

Farewell!—This letter will be to your taste, it is full of factual accounts.

22 May

That the life of Man is but a dream has been sensed by many a one, and I too am never free of the feeling. When I consider the restrictions that are placed on the active, inquiring energies of Man; when I see that all our efforts have no other result than to satisfy needs which in turn serve no purpose but to prolong our wretched existence, and then see that all our reassurance concerning the particular questions we probe is no more than a dreamy resignation, since all we are doing is to paint our prison walls with colourful figures and bright views—all of this, Wilhelm, leaves me silent. I withdraw into myself, and discover a world, albeit a notional world of dark desire rather than one of actuality and vital strength. And everything swims before my senses, and I go my way in the world wearing the smile of the dreamer.

All our learned teachers and educators are agreed that children do not know why they want what they want; but no one is willing to believe that adults too, like children, wander about this earth in a daze and, like children, do not know where they come from or where they are going, act as rarely as they do according to genuine motives, and are as thoroughly governed as they are by biscuits and cake and the rod. And yet it seems palpably clear to me.

I gladly confess, since I know the reply you would want to make, that they are the happiest who, like children, live for the present moment, drag their dolls around and dress and undress them, and watchfully steal by the drawer where Mama has locked away the cake, and, when at last they get their hands on what they want, devour it with their cheeks crammed full and cry, 'More!'—They are happy creatures. And those others, who give pompous titles to their beggarly pursuits and even to their passions, and chalk them up as vast enterprises for the good and well-being of mankind, they too are happy.—It is all very well for those who can be like that! But he who humbly perceives where it is all leading, who sees how prettily the happy man makes an Eden of his garden, and how even the unhappy man goes willingly on his weary way, panting beneath his burden, and that all are equally interested in seeing the light of the sun for one minute more—he indeed will be silent, and will create a world from within for himself, and be happy because he is a man. And then, confined as he may be, he none the less still preserves in his heart the sweet sensation of freedom, and the knowledge that he can quit this prison whenever he wishes.

26 May

You know of old my way of making myself a home, of pitching my humble shelter in some pleasant place and lodging there in the most modest of manners. Here too I have once again been attracted to such a spot.

About an hour outside the town is a place they call Wahlheim.*[12] It is most engagingly situated on a hill, and when you are up above and following the path out of the village you suddenly have a view across the entire valley. A kindly innkeeper, obliging and cheerful in her old age, has wine, beer and coffee to offer; and best of all are the two linden trees whose spreading boughs shade the little church square, which is surrounded by farmers' houses, barns and yards. It has not been easy to find so pleasant and cosy a spot; and now I have my little table and my chair carried out of the inn, and drink my coffee there, and read my Homer. The first time I walked beneath these lindens, by chance one beautiful afternoon, I found the square perfectly deserted. Everyone was out in the fields except a boy about four years old who was sitting on the ground and holding another child of perhaps six months that sat between his feet; he was holding it to his breast with both arms, so that he served as a kind of armchair; and, despite the vivacity that sparkled in his black eyes as he gazed around, he sat quite tranquilly. The sight delighted me: I sat down on a plough across from them, and took great pleasure in drawing this brotherly picture. I added the fence that was near them, a barn door and a few broken cart-wheels, all simply the way it was, and after an hour I found I had produced a harmoniously correct and arresting drawing without putting into it anything whatsoever of my own. This confirmed me in my resolve to keep to Nature alone in future. Only Nature has inexhaustible riches, and only Nature creates a great artist. A good deal can be said of the advantages of rules, much the same as can be said in praise of bourgeois society. A man shaped by the rules will never produce anything tasteless or bad, just as a citizen who observes laws and decorum will never be an unbearable neighbour or an out-and-out villain; and yet on the other hand, say what you please, the rules will destroy the true feeling of Nature and its true expression! You may say: 'You are too hard! The rules merely contain, they cut back the ranker growth, etc.'—My good friend, let me offer you an analogy. It is the same as it is with love. A young fellow is totally infatuated with a girl, spends every hour of the day

* The reader need go to no lengths to locate the places mentioned here; it has been considered necessary to alter the actual names given in the original text.

32

with her, wears himself out and squanders his fortune to give her constant proof that his devotion to her knows no end. And then some philistine, some man of public rank, comes and says to him: 'My dear young sir! To love is only natural, but you must be true to human nature when you love! Divide up your hours, some for your work and some for recreation with your girl. Calculate your income and, once your necessities are seen to, I shall be the last to urge against giving her a present with what remains, though not too often: on her birthday, say, or her saint's day.' And so forth.—If the man obeys, he will turn out a respectable young chap, and I should personally advise any prince to appoint him to his council; but his love will be done for, and so, if he is an artist, will his art. Oh, my friends! You ask why the torrent of genius so rarely pours forth, so rarely floods and thunders and overwhelms your astonished soul?—Because, dear friends, on either bank dwell the cool, respectable gentlemen, whose summer-houses, tulip beds and cabbage patches would all be washed away, and who are therefore highly skilled in averting future dangers in good time, by damming and digging channels.

27 May

I see that I have fallen into raptures, parables and declamation, and in the process have forgotten to tell you the rest of the story concerning the children. I sat there on my plough for a good two hours, quite absorbed in those painter's sensations I told you of, in a highly piecemeal way, in yesterday's letter. Towards evening a young woman carrying a little basket approached the children, who had not made a move the whole time, and called from a distance: 'Philipps, you are a very good boy.'—She wished me good day, I thanked her, stood up and crossed closer, and asked if she was the mother of the children? She said she was, and, giving the eldest half a roll, picked up the little one and kissed him with motherly love.—'I gave Philipps the little one to look after,' she said, 'while I went into town with my eldest boy to buy white bread and sugar and an earthenware pot.'—I could see all of that in the basket, the cover of which had slipped off.—'I am going to cook some soup for Hans' (that was the name of the

33

youngest) 'this evening; this reckless chap, the big one, broke my pot yesterday when he and Philipps were squabbling over the pot-scrapings.'—I asked about the eldest, and she had scarcely told me that he was chasing some geese around the meadow but he came bounding up, bringing a hazel switch for the second oldest. I went on talking to the woman and gathered that she was the schoolmaster's daughter and that her husband was away on a journey to Switzerland to collect a cousin's inheritance.—'They tried to cheat him out of it,' she said, 'and did not reply to his letters, so he has gone himself. I only hope he has not had an accident. I have heard nothing from him.'—Reluctantly I took my leave of the woman, giving a kreutzer to each of the children and her one for the youngest too, so that she could buy it a roll to go with the soup when next she went to town; and so we parted.

I tell you, my precious friend, whenever my mind is tottering all the tumult is soothed to quiet by the sight of a creature like this, living in the small daily round of her existence in a state of happy tranquillity, getting by from one day to the next, seeing the leaves fall and thinking nothing but that winter is coming.

Since then I have often been out there. The children have grown quite used to me, they get sugar when I drink my coffee and in the evenings they share my sandwiches and soured milk. On Sundays they never lack for a kreutzer, and, if I am not there after vespers, the inn-woman has instructions to pay it out.

They are on intimate terms with me, tell me all manner of things, and I take particular delight in their passions and simple cravings, once a number of the village children are together.

I have been at great pains to disabuse their mother of her concern that they might be inconveniencing the gentleman.

30 May

What I told you recently concerning painting is doubtless also true of poetry: what counts is that one perceives excellence and dares to give it expression, which sounds little but is in fact a great deal. Today I witnessed a scene which, if written down plainly and exactly, would

34

be the loveliest idyll the world has ever seen; but why trouble with poetry and scenes and idylls? Must we go tinkering about with Nature before we can enjoy it?

If you are expecting a lot of loftiness and elegance after this introduction, you have been sorely deceived once again; it is merely a farmer lad that has prompted such lively interest. As usual I shall tell it poorly, and I suppose that you, as usual, will consider I exaggerate; and again it is Wahlheim, always Wahlheim, that supplies these curiosities.

A party was outside under the lindens, taking coffee. Since they were not the fittest of company, I made an excuse and stayed away.

A farmer lad came out of one of the neighbouring houses and busied himself making some repair to the plough I had recently drawn. I liked his way, so I spoke to him and asked after his circumstances, and presently we were acquainted and soon, as generally happens to me with this kind of person, intimate. He told me that he was in service with a widow, and very well cared for by her. He spoke of her so much, and praised her so highly, that I soon realized he was devoted to her body and soul. She was no longer young, he said, and had been badly treated by her first husband, so that she did not want to remarry; and from his account it was so apparent that he found her beautiful and charming, and ardently wished she might choose him to erase the memory of her first husband's errors, that I should have to repeat his every word to convey this man's pure affection, his love, his devotion. Indeed, I should need the gifts of the greatest of poets if I were also to describe his expressive gestures, the harmony of his voice and the secret fire in his eyes, to any effect. No, there are no words for the tenderness that was in his entire being, his every expression; everything I could say would only be crude. I was particularly touched by his fear lest I think his relationship to his mistress a dishonourable one or doubt the propriety of her conduct. How delightful it was when he spoke of her figure, her person, which, without the graces of youth, attracted him powerfully and won him: all I can do is re-live it in my inmost soul. Never in my life have I witnessed (or, I might add, even conceived or dreamt of) intense desire and burning, ardent longing of such purity. Bear with me when I tell you that when I recall this innocence and truth my very soul is afire, and that the image of his devotion and tenderness follows me wherever I go, and that, as if kindled by it myself, I am all longing and languishing.

I shall now try to see her too as soon as possible, or rather, on second thoughts, I shall avoid doing so. It is better for me to see her with the eyes of her lover; perhaps she would not appear to my own eyes as she does now, and why should I ruin the beautiful image I have?

16 June

Why I have not written to you?—You, who are a learned man too, ask a question like that. You might guess that things are well with me, and indeed—In a word, I have made an acquaintance who has touched my heart very closely. I have—I know not what.

I shall scarcely be able to tell you how I grew acquainted with one of the most lovable of creatures. I am in good spirits, and happy, and therefore not the best of storytellers.

An angel!—Rot!—Every man says that about his beloved, does he not? And yet I am unable to tell you how, and why, she is perfection itself; suffice to say that she has captivated me utterly.

So much simplicity with so much understanding, so much goodness and so much resolve, and tranquillity of soul together with true life and vitality.—

Everything I am telling you about her is fearful twaddle, tiresome abstractions that do not express a single trait of her being. Some other time—no, not another time, I shall tell it you right now. If I don't do so now I never will. For, between ourselves, since I started writing I have already been three times on the point of laying down my pen, having my horse saddled and riding out. And yet I vowed this morning that I would not go riding, and none the less I go to the window every moment or so to see how high the sun still is.—

I couldn't resist it. I had to go to see her. Here I am again, Wilhelm, about to eat my supper and write to you. What joy it is for my soul, to see her amidst those dear, cheerful children, her eight brothers and sisters!—

If I go on like this you will know as much when I am through as you did at the start. So lend an ear and I shall force myself to give you the details.

Recently I wrote that I had become acquainted with S., the estate officer, who invited me to visit him soon at his retreat, or rather in his little kingdom. I neglected to do so, and perhaps would never have gone if chance had not revealed to me the treasure that lies concealed in those peaceful parts.

The young people here had arranged a ball out in the country,[13] and I gladly agreed to be one of the party. I asked one of the local girls, a good, pretty and otherwise insignificant girl, to be my companion; and we planned that I should take a carriage and drive out to the scene of the festivities with my dancing partner and her aunt, picking up Charlotte S.[14] on the way.—'You will be getting to know a beautiful young woman,' my companion informed me as we drove through the vast wooded park to the hunting lodge.—'Be on your guard,' put in the aunt, 'and take care not to fall in love!'—'Why?' I asked.—'She is already promised to a very worthy man,' she replied, 'who has gone away to put his affairs in order following the death of his father, and to see about a decent position.'—This information left me pretty much indifferent.

The sun was still a quarter hour from touching the mountains as we drove up at the gate of the courtyard. It was very sultry, and the ladies voiced fears of the thunderstorm that appeared to be approaching on the horizon, where dank whitish-grey clouds were gathering. I set their minds at rest by affecting expertise in matters of the weather, though all the time I was myself beginning to suspect that our pleasures would be dealt a blow.

I had got down, and the maid who came to the gate asked for a moment's indulgence, and said Mamsell' Lottchen would be with us right away. I crossed the courtyard to a well-built house and, climbing the flight of steps in front, opened the door and beheld the most charming scene I have ever set eyes on. In the hallway, six children aged between eleven and two were milling about a girl with a wonderful figure and of medium height, wearing a simple white dress with pink ribbons at the sleeves and breast. She was holding a loaf of rye bread and cutting a piece for each of the little ones about her, according to their age and appetite;[15] she handed out the slices with great kindliness, and the children reached up their little hands long before the bread was cut, cried out their artless thanks and then either bounded away contented with their supper or, in the case of the quieter ones, walked tranquilly out to the courtyard gate to look at the strangers and the carriage in which their Lotte was to drive away. —'Do forgive me for putting you to the trouble of coming in,' she said, 'and for keeping the ladies waiting. What with dressing, and seeing that all will be well in the house in my absence, I forgot to give my children their supper, and they won't have their bread cut by anyone but me.'—I paid her some unimportant compliment; my entire soul was transfixed by her figure, her tone, her manner, and I barely had time to recover from my surprise when she ran into the parlour to fetch her gloves and fan. The little ones gazed at me from a distance, with sideways glances, and I went up to the youngest, a child with the happiest of features. He was just shying away as Lotte re-entered and said: 'Louis, shake your cousin's hand.'—The lad did so very willingly, and, in spite of his runny little nose, I could not resist giving him a hearty kiss.—'Cousin?' I asked, offering her my hand. 'Do you really think me worthy of the happy fortune of being related to you?'—'Oh,' she said, with an easy smile, 'we have a lot of cousins, and I should be sorry to think you the worst of them.'—As she left she told Sophie, a girl of about eleven and the eldest sister after herself, to take good care of the children and to give her love to Papa when he returned from his ride. To the little ones she said that they were to obey their sister Sophie as if it were herself, and some of them expressly promised to do so. However, one cheeky little blonde girl of about six said: 'But she isn't you, Lottchen, and we like you more.'—The two eldest boys had clambered onto the back of the carriage, and at my request she allowed them to ride with us as far as the woods, as long as they promised not to get up to any mischief and to hold on tight.

We had scarcely settled in our seats, and the ladies had hardly greeted each other, passed comments on each other's attire and especially their hats, and made the usual review of the company that was expected, than Lotte had the coachman stop and her brothers get down; they then desired to kiss her hand once again, which the elder did with all the tenderness of a fifteen-year-old and the other with considerable vehemence and abandon. She sent her love to the little ones once again, and we drove on.

The aunt asked if she had finished the book she had recently sent her.—'No,' said Lotte, 'I do not like it, you can have it back. The one before was no better, either.'—I was astounded on asking which books they were and being told——.* —I found great character in everything she said, and with every word I saw fresh charms and radiance of spirit brightening her features, which gradually took on a contented appearance since she could feel that I understood her.

'When I was younger,' she said, 'there was nothing I loved better than novels. God knows how good it felt to be able to sit in some corner on a Sunday and share with my whole heart in Miss Jenny's[16] happiness and sorrows. Nor do I deny that that kind of writing still has its charms for me. But since I so rarely come by a book, it has to be one that is quite to my taste. And I like that author best who shows me my own world, conditions such as I live in myself, and a story that can engage my interest and heart as much as my own domestic life does, which is certainly no paradise but is still on the whole a source of inexpressible happiness.'

I tried to conceal the moving effect these words had on me. True, I was not able to do so for long; for as soon as I heard her speak in passing, with such truth, of *The Vicar of Wakefield*,[17] and of——,†[18] I could no longer contain myself, told her everything I had to say, and only after some time had passed, when Lotte included the others in the conversation, did I notice that they had been sitting there goggle-eyed the whole while and behaving as if they were not there at all. On several occasions the aunt looked at me with a derisive twitch of the nose, but I cared nothing for that.

The talk turned to the pleasures of dancing.—'Even if it is wrong to have a passion for it,' said Lotte, 'I gladly confess that there is nothing I like better than dancing. And if I am worried about something, I hammer out a country dance on my out-of-tune piano, and everything is all right again.'

Knowing me as you do, you can imagine how I delighted in her

* It has been thought necessary to suppress this passage in the letter, so that no one may have cause for complaint; though at bottom the opinion of some girl or of a young unstable man can mean little to any author.
† Here too the names of a number of our fatherland's authors have been omitted. Those to whom Lotte's applause is due will doubtless feel it in their hearts on reading this passage, and no one else need know.

dark eyes during this conversation, how my entire soul was drawn to her young lips and fresh, bright cheeks and how I was so absorbed in the splendid meaning of her words that I scarcely registered the way she expressed herself. In short, when we drew up before the house I got down from the carriage as if in a dream, and was so lost in dreams in that dusky world that I hardly heard the music that sounded across from the brightly lit ballroom above.

Mr Audran and a certain N.N.—who can remember all these names?—who were the aunt's and Lotte's partners, met us at the carriage door and took charge of their ladies, and I led my own up and in.

We twined about each other in minuets; I asked one lady after another for a dance, and of course the most unbearable of all could not bring themselves to offer their hands and leave off. Lotte and her partner began an English country dance, and you can imagine how good I felt when it was their turn to dance the figure in our row. You should see her dance! Her whole heart and soul are in it, you see, and her body is all harmony, so carefree and relaxed, as if there were nothing else, as if she had not a single other thought or sensation; and, in that moment, undoubtedly everything else ceases to exist for her.

I asked her for the second country dance; she promised me the third, and assured me with the most engaging openness that she loved dancing the *allemande*.—'It is the custom here,' she went on, 'for couples that are together to dance the *allemande* together, but my partner is a poor waltzer and will be grateful if I relieve him of his duty. Your lady cannot do it either and does not care for it, but I noticed during the English country dance that you waltz well; so if you would like to be my partner for the *allemande*, I suggest you request it of my gentleman, and I shall propose it to your lady.'—We shook hands on this, and arranged that her partner should entertain mine in the meantime.

Now things really started, and for a while we took delight in the various graceful motions of our arms. What grace and ease were in her movements! We now began to waltz, sweeping about one another like the spheres, and it was, I grant, pretty confused at the outset, since very few were able to dance it properly. We had our wits about us and let the rest wear themselves out, and when the clumsiest of

40

them had quit the floor we fell to and acquitted ourselves famously alongside another couple, Audran and his partner. Never in all my life have I danced so well. I was no longer a mere mortal. Holding the most adorable of creatures in my arms and flying about with her like lightning, so that I forgot everything about me, and—Wilhelm, to be honest, I swore that a girl I loved and had a claim on should never waltz with anyone but me, not even if it cost me my life. You take my meaning!

We took a few turns about the ballroom to recover our breath. Then she sat down, and was most refreshed by the oranges I had put aside and which were now the only ones left; though every piece she politely shared with the greedy woman beside her put a dagger through my heart.

We were the second couple in the third English country dance. As we were going down the row, and I, with God knows how great an ecstasy, was gazing at her arms and eyes, which were alive with the warmth of the purest, most genuine pleasure, we passed a woman who had struck me on account of her amiable expression, though her face was no longer quite young. She looked at Lotte with a smile, raised a warning finger, and as she flew by uttered the name Albert, twice and in a very significant tone.

'Who is Albert?' I said to Lotte, 'if it is not impertinent to ask.'—She was about to answer when we were obliged to separate to dance the grand figure of eight; and I thought I saw signs of pensiveness on her brow as we crossed each other's paths.—'Why should I hide it from you?' she said, as she gave me her hand for the promenade. 'Albert[19] is a dear, honest man to whom I am as good as engaged.'—Now this was no news to me (since the girls had told me on the way), yet none the less, it was utterly new to me as I had not yet connected the thought with her, who had come in so short a time to mean so much to me. In brief, I was confused, forgot what I was at, and blundered into the wrong couple, so that everything was in disarray and Lotte's entire presence of mind and tugging and pulling were needed to restore a hasty order.

The dance had not yet finished when the lightning, which we had seen flaring on the horizon for some time and which I had pronounced to be merely sheet lightning, began to flash more violently, and the thunder to drown out the music. Three ladies fled the rows,

41

followed by their gentlemen; the confusion became general, and the music ceased. If something distressing or terrible surprises us in our pleasures, it naturally makes a more powerful impression on us than at other times, partly because the contrast affects us very keenly, and partly and more importantly because our senses have been opened to feelings and we are the more susceptible to impressions. To such causes I must ascribe the remarkable grimaces made by several of the ladies. The cleverest sat in a corner, her back to the window, and held her hands over her ears. A second knelt before her and buried her head in the first lady's lap. A third shoved in between the two of them and embraced her little sisters, shedding a thousand tears. Some wanted to go home; others, still less aware of what they were about, did not even have the presence of mind to rein in their young gallants, who seemed extremely busy lapping up fearful prayers from the lips of the lovely unfortunates, prayers intended for heaven. Some of the gentlemen had gone downstairs to smoke a pipe in peace and quiet; and, when the hostess had the bright idea of suggesting moving to a room with shutters and curtains, none of the rest rejected her offer. We were scarcely there but Lotte was busy setting out a circle of chairs, and, once the company was seated as she requested, she proposed that we play a game.

I saw one or two of the gentlemen licking their lips and stretching their limbs in hopes of some delicious forfeit.—'Let's play counting!' she said. 'Listen carefully! I shall go round the circle anti-clockwise, and you all keep count, everyone saying his number in turn, but at top speed, mind, and anyone who hesitates or says the wrong number gets a clip round the ear, and so on up to a thousand.'—It was a hilarious sight. She went round the circle with her arm stretched out. 'One,' began the first; 'two,' said his neighbour; 'three,' the next; and so forth. Then she began to go faster, and faster, till one missed his number: smack! his ears were boxed, and amidst the laughter came the next smack! And ever faster. I myself was slapped twice, and took great pleasure in supposing them heartier slaps than she gave the others. The game dissolved into all-round laughter and merriment before we had reached a thousand. Those who were intimate withdrew separately; the storm had passed over, and I followed Lotte into the ballroom. On the way, she said: 'Boxing their ears put the storm and everything clean out of their minds!'—I could make no

42

reply.—'I was one of the most afraid myself,' she continued, 'and in pretending to be brave, to stiffen the others' courage, I found my own courage.'—We went to the window. The thunder was passing by and a wonderful rain was falling on the land, filling the warm air with the most refreshing fragrance. She stood there resting on her elbows, gazing deep into the country about us; she looked to the heavens, and at me, and I saw there were tears in her eyes; and she laid her hand on mine and said, 'Klopstock!'[20] At once I remembered the glorious ode she had in mind, and was lost in the sensations that flooded me on hearing the name. It was more than I could bear; I bowed over her hand and kissed it, shedding tears of the greatest joy, and once again looked up to gaze into her eyes—Noble poet! if only you had seen the adoration of you in those eyes! and if only I might never hear again your oft-profaned name!

19 June

I no longer recall where I had got to in my story the other day; all I know is that it was two in the morning before I was in bed, and if I had had you here to talk to, instead of writing, I might well have kept you up until daybreak.

What happened during the drive home from the ball I have not yet told you, nor have I the time to do so today.

It was the most marvellous of sunrises. Raindrops were dripping in the woods and the countryside all around us was refreshed! Our lady companions fell asleep. She asked me if I did not want to follow suit, and said I should not stand on ceremony on her account.—'As long as your own eyes are open,' I replied, gazing evenly at her, 'there is little chance of my sleeping.'—And we both remained awake as far as her gate, where the maid quietly opened up and, in answer to her questions, assured her that her father and the little ones were well, and all still asleep. I took my leave of her, first asking if I might see her later the same day; she consented, and I went—and since then the sun and moon and stars can go about their business as they please, but as for me, I do not know if it is day or night, and the whole world is as nothing to me.

My days are as happy as any God sets aside for his saints; and, whatever the future may have in store for me, I cannot claim I have not enjoyed the pleasures of life, the very purest of pleasures.—You know my Wahlheim; I am quite at home there now, and from there it is only half an hour to Lotte, and there I take pleasure in myself and all the happiness that can be Man's.

I scarcely thought, when I chose Wahlheim as a place to walk to, that it was so close to heaven! How often on my rambles, from a hilltop or from the flatland across the river, have I seen the hunting lodge where all my longings lie!

Dear Wilhelm, I have thought a great deal about Man's desire to go out into the world, make new discoveries and go a-wandering; and, on the other hand, about that deep-seated impulse to be contented with limits that are imposed, and gladly to proceed as custom dictates, with no interest in what goes on beyond the daily round.

When I first came here and looked down into that lovely valley from the hill, the way the entire scene charmed me was a marvel. —That little wood!—Ah, if only you might walk in its shade!—That mountain-top!—Ah, to view this vast landscape from there!—And the chain of hills, and the gentle valleys!—Oh, to lose myself amongst them!—And I hastened there, and returned without having found what I was hoping for. Oh, distance is like the future: before our souls lies an entire and dusky vastness which overwhelms our feelings as it overwhelms our eyes, and ah! we long to surrender the whole of our being, and be filled with all the joy of one single, immense, magnificent emotion.—And then, ah! once we hasten onwards, and what lay ahead becomes the here and now, everything is just as it was, and there we are, as poor and confined as ever, our souls longing for the elusive balm.

In the same way, the most restless of travellers ends up pining for his homeland once again, and discovers in his cottage, in the arms of his wife and amidst his children, and in the labours that are necessary to support them, that joy he sought in vain in the wide world.

In the mornings I go out to Wahlheim at sunrise, pick *mange-tout* in the innkeeper's garden and sit down to trim them, now and then reading my Homer, and choose a pot in the little kitchen, scoop out the butter, put the peas on the heat and cover them and sit by them to give them an occasional stir; and when I do all this I can feel quite keenly how Penelope's ruffianly suitors slaughter, dress and roast their oxen and swine.[21] Nothing gives me so true and restful an emotion as the manners of patriarchal life, which (thank God) I can make a part of my own way of life without any affectation.

It is good that my heart can feel the simple and innocent pleasure a man knows when the cabbage he eats at table is one he grew himself; the pleasure he takes not only in eating the cabbage but in remembering all those good days, the fine morning he planted it, the mellow evenings he watered it and the delight he felt in its daily growth.

29 June

The day before yesterday the physician came out from town to visit the estate officer and found me on the floor with Lotte's children, some of them climbing on top of me, some of them poking me, and me tickling them, and all of us yelling our heads off. The doctor is a pedantic jack-fool of a fellow who is forever folding the frills on his cuffs while he is talking and plucking forth some endlessly long ruffle, and considered my conduct beneath the dignity of sensible people; I could tell by his nose. But I did not let it bother me, and while he held forth in his immensely rational way I rebuilt the card-houses the children had knocked down. Whereupon he went about town afterwards complaining that the officer's children are spoilt enough as it is, and now Werther is ruining them completely.

Yes, my dear Wilhelm, nothing on earth is closer to my heart than children. When I watch them and see in the smallest of creatures the seeds of all the virtues and strengths they will one day need so badly; when I see their obstinacy as future resolution and firmness of character, and their caprice as good humour and that light touch which makes it easy to negotiate the troubles of life, and all of it so unspoilt, so intact!—I always, always call to mind the golden words of Man's teacher: 'Except ye become as little children'![22]—And yet,

45

dear friend, we treat them as our subjects, these children who are our equals and whom we ought to consider as models. We claim they have no will of their own!—Do we have none, then? and why should we have an exclusive right to a will?—Because we are older and wiser!—Dear God, when Thou lookest down from heaven, all Thou seest is old children and young; and Thy Son long since declared which of them give Thee the greater joy. But they believe in Him and do not listen to His words—that too is an old story!—and they make their children in their own images, and—Adieu, Wilhelm! I shall blether about it no more.

1 July

The solace Lotte affords the sick I can feel in my own poor heart, which is in a worse way than many a patient ailing on a sickbed. She is to spend a few days in town with a worthy woman who is near to death, according to the doctors, and who wishes to have Lotte with her in her last moments. Last week I went with her to call on the vicar of S., a village away in the hills, an hour's journey. We arrived shortly before four o'clock. Lotte had taken her second-oldest sister with her. When we entered the vicarage courtyard, under the shade of two tall walnut trees, the good old man was sitting on a bench outside the front door, and on seeing Lotte he seemed to gain new life and, rising and forgetting his gnarled walking-stick, ventured towards her. She ran to him and made him sit down, sitting beside him herself, passed on her father's good wishes, and hugged his youngest boy, a nasty, dirty lad and the joy of his old age. You should have seen the way she kept him amused, raising her voice because he is half deaf, telling him of young, healthy people who had died unexpectedly, singing the praises of Karlsbad and commending his decision to go there next summer, and saying she thought he looked a lot better and livelier than the last time she had seen him.—In the meantime I had paid my compliments to the vicar's wife. The old man grew quite high-spirited, and, as I could not help admiring the beautiful walnut trees which shaded us so delightfully, he began to tell us their story, albeit with some difficulty.—'That old one,' he said, 'we don't know who planted that one. Some say it was one vicar and some say another. But the younger one over there is as old as my wife, fifty years old come October. Her father planted it in the morning, and that same evening she was born. He was my predecessor here, and I cannot tell you how fond he was of that tree; and I'm sure I am every bit as fond of it myself. The very first time I set foot in this courtyard, twenty-seven years ago, when I was a poor student, my wife was sitting on a log beneath that tree, knitting.'—Lotte inquired after his daughter; he replied that she had gone with Mr Schmidt to see the farmworkers in the meadows. Then the old man went on with his story, telling us how his predecessor had taken a liking to him, as had his daughter, and how he had become his curate and subsequently his successor. He had barely finished his tale when his daughter returned through the garden, with the Mr Schmidt we had heard of; she gave Lotte a warm and hearty welcome, and I must say I found her quite attractive: a lively, well-built brunette, who would have entertained one very nicely for a short while in the country. Mr Schmidt proved to be her beloved and was a polite but reserved fellow, reluctant to join in our conversation, though Lotte repeatedly tried to include him. I was particularly vexed to gather from his facial expression that what prevented him from speaking was not want of wit but rather a perverse ill-humour. Unfortunately this turned out all too plainly to be the fact of the matter; as we took a walk, and Friederike joined Lotte and at times me as well, the gentleman's countenance, which was a rather dark shade anyway, visibly turned a more sombre colour, till Lotte tugged at my sleeve and informed me that I had been getting on too well by half with Friederike. Now there is nothing I find more irritating than when people torment each other, and it is worst of all when young people in their prime, who might be enjoying all the pleasures life offers, ruin the few sunny days they have by pulling miserable faces, and never realize the error of their ways till it is too late to do anything about it. It annoyed me; and towards evening, when we had returned to the vicarage and were sitting at table eating bread and milk, and the talk was of the joys and sorrows of the world, I could not help seizing on the subject and making a hearty speech against ill-humour.—'We often complain that there are so few good days and so many bad ones,' I began, 'but I think we are wrong to do so. If our hearts were always open, so that we could enjoy the good things God bestows on us every day, we should also have the strength to bear the misfortunes that come our way.'—'But we cannot control our dispositions,' countered the vicar's wife; 'so much depends on the body! If we feel unwell, nothing will please us.'—I conceded the point.—'In that case,' I continued, 'let us consider ill-humour a disease, and inquire whether there is no remedy for it.'—'I should be glad to hear of one,' said Lotte. 'I for one believe a great deal depends on ourselves. That is how it is with me. If something is annoying and dispiriting me, I leap up and sing a few country dance tunes in the garden, and feel better in no time at all.'—'That is exactly what I was trying to say,' I replied. 'Ill-humour is just like indolence; in fact it is a kind of indolence. We are inclined that way by nature, but if we only have the strength to pull ourselves together our work goes wonderfully and we take real pleasure in what we are doing.'—Friederike was paying close attention; and the young fellow objected that we are not our own masters and are far from being able to govern our feelings.—'We are talking about an unpleasant feeling that everyone prefers to be rid of,' I answered, 'and no one knows the extent of his own powers till he has tested them. The sick will consult any number of doctors, after all, and will submit to the strictest regimen and swallow the bitterest pills, to be restored to health as they wish.'—I noticed that the venerable old gentleman was straining to hear, in order to follow our discussion, so I raised my voice and spoke directly to him. 'We hear sermons against so many evils,' I said, 'but I have never heard of anyone preaching against ill-humour from the pulpit.'*—'You must get your town ministers to do that,' said he, 'because farmers are never out of humour; though it mightn't do any harm at times, as a lesson for my wife or the estate officer, at any rate.'—We all laughed, and he laughed heartily too till he fell into a coughing fit, which interrupted our debate for a while; then the young fellow resumed the subject. 'You called ill-humour an evil; I feel that is overstated.'—'Not at all,' I replied, 'if things that do harm to oneself and one's neighbours deserve the name of evil. Is it not enough that we are unable to make each other happy? Must we also

* In Lavater's collection of sermons on the Book of Jonah we now have an excellent sermon on this subject.[23]

48

rob each other of the pleasure our hearts can all still give at times? Just show me the man who is out of humour but has the decency to conceal the fact and bear his ill-temper alone without destroying the happiness of those about him! Is not ill-humour in fact our own inner displeasure at our own unworthiness, a feeling of discontent with ourselves, which is always related to envy, which in turn is stirred up by foolish vanity? We see people who are happy and whose happiness is not of our making, and we cannot stand it.'—Lotte smiled at me, seeing the emotion with which I spoke, and a tear in Friederike's eye prompted me to go on.—'Woe betide those,' I said, 'who use the power they have over someone's heart to rob it of the simple joys that are in its nature. All the presents and attentions in the world cannot make up for that moment of natural pleasure that the tyrant's envious cruelty has soured.'

My whole heart was full at that moment; the recollection of various events in the past pressed upon my soul, and tears came to my eyes.

'Every day we should remind ourselves,' I exclaimed, 'that there is nothing we can do for our friends but to leave them their pleasures and to increase their happiness by enjoying it with them. When their inmost souls are tormented by terrifying passion or torn with grief, can you afford them the slightest consolation? And then, when the last and most dreadful sickness seizes the creature you weakened in her prime, and she lies there wretched and exhausted, her dim eyes raised to heaven, the fever of death on her pale brow, and you stand by the bedside like a soul damned—then you sense deep down that your entire fortune cannot help her, and you are convulsed by the fearful thought that you would give everything to give this failing creature just a little strength, just a scrap of courage.'

As I said these words, the recollection of a similar scene I had once been present at overwhelmed me totally. Holding my handkerchief to my eyes, I left the room, and did not recover my self-possession until I heard Lotte's voice, calling that it was time to go. And how she chided me, on the way home, for becoming too heatedly involved in everything! She said it would be the end of me, and I should spare myself!—What an angel! I shall live for you!

She is still with her dying friend, and is still the same helpful, dear creature, alleviating pain and shedding happiness wherever she turns. Yesterday evening she went for a walk with Marianne and little Malchen;[24] I knew they intended to do so, met them, and we walked together. An hour and a half later we returned to the town past the spring I love so much and which is a thousand times dearer to me now. Lotte sat down on the low wall and we stood by her. I looked around, and ah, the time when my heart was so alone returned to me.—'Dear spring,' I said, 'since then I have not rested here where it is cool any more, and at times as I hastened by I have not even looked your way.'—I glanced down and saw that Malchen was climbing the steps, holding a glass of water very intently.—I looked at Lotte and was filled with a sense of her virtues. By now Malchen had reached us with the glass. Marianne was about to take it from her: 'No!' cried the child, with the sweetest of expressions. 'No, you have to drink first, Lottchen.'—The natural and good-natured way she called this out delighted me so much that I could express my emotion in no other way than by picking up the child and kissing her heartily, whereupon she instantly started to shriek and cry.—'That was wrong of you,' Lotte said.—I was embarrassed.—'Come on, Malchen,' she went on, taking the child by the hand and leading her down the flight of steps, 'quickly, come on and wash your face with fresh spring water, quickly, then it won't have any effect.'—And so I stood there watching as the child wet her hands and furiously rubbed her cheeks, believing absolutely that the wondrous spring would wash away all the contamination and the ignominy of growing an ugly beard—and Lotte said, 'That's enough!' but still the child went on busily rubbing, as if to make doubly sure—and I assure you, Wilhelm, I have never attended a baptism with greater reverence; and when Lotte ascended the steps I would have liked to prostrate myself before her, as before some prophet who has taken away the sins of a nation.

That evening, my heart full of joy, I could not resist describing the incident to a man I supposed had some feeling for human nature since he is a man of sense; but what a reception I met with! He said it was very bad of Lotte; that it was wrong to encourage nonsensical beliefs in children; that it led to countless errors and superstitions, which one ought to protect children from in good time.—At this I recalled that the man had had a child baptized a week ago, so I let it pass, preserving the truth in my own heart: we should treat children as God treats us; He makes us happiest when He leaves us our pleasant delusions.

8 July

What a child one is![25] How one can be so hungry for a look! What a child one is!—We had been to Wahlheim. The ladies took a carriage, and while we were out walking I thought I saw in Lotte's dark eyes—I am a fool, forgive me! but you should see those eyes—To be brief about it, then (for my eyelids are heavy with sleep): there we were, the ladies getting in, and young W., Selstadt, Audran and I standing by the carriage. The ladies backchatted from the carriage door with us chaps, and to be sure we were the soul of lighthearted merriment.—I tried to catch Lotte's eyes; but ah, they gazed from one to another! but not at me! me! me! The only one there who saw nothing but her, and she did not look my way!—My heart bade her a thousand adieus! And she did not see me! The carriage drove off, and my eyes filled with tears. I looked after it, and saw Lotte's bonnet leaning out of the window, and she turned to look back, ah! at me!—My dear fellow, that is the uncertainty I am left in; and my consolation is that perhaps she did turn to look at me! Perhaps!—Good night! Oh, what a child I am!

10 July

You should see what an oaf I look if her name is mentioned in company! Especially if someone asks me how I like her.—Like her! I utterly detest the word. What kind of man would merely like Lotte, and not have all his senses and feelings dominated by her! Like her! Recently some fellow asked me how I liked Ossian![26]

Mrs M. is in a very bad way; I pray for her, and share in Lotte's sufferings. I see her on occasion at a friend's house, and today she told me something quite remarkable.—Old M. is a greedy, miserly peasant, and has filled his wife's life with torments and restrictions; but the woman has always managed to get by. A few days ago, when the doctor had announced there was no hope of her recovering, she sent for her husband (Lotte was in the room) and spoke to him in this way: 'I have something to confess to you which might cause confusion and embarrassment after my death. I have always kept this household in as orderly and thrifty a way as was possible, but you will have to forgive me: for the last thirty years I have been deceiving you. When our married life began, you fixed a small amount for kitchen and other household expenses. As our household grew and our property grew larger, you could not be moved to increase my weekly allowance in proportion to our requirements. To be brief, you well know that in times when our needs were greatest you demanded I should manage on seven florins a week. I took the seven florins without comment and made up the weekly deficit out of our takings, since no one would suspect your wife of robbing our money-chest. I wasted nothing, and would gladly have met my eternal maker without confessing it, if it weren't that whoever manages this household after I am gone would be at a loss, and you would be forever insisting that your first wife got by on that amount.'

I talked to Lotte about the unbelievable ways that Man can be deluded; how a man might not suspect there was more to things than met the eye when he allowed seven florins to cover expenses that were maybe twice as great. But I have myself known people who would readily and without any surprise have imagined their house had the prophet's never-failing cruse of oil.[27]

No, I am not deceiving myself! I can read a genuine interest in me and my fate in those dark eyes of hers. Yes, I can feel—and I know I may trust my own heart in this—Oh, dare I utter the words, those words that contain all heaven for me?—I can feel that she loves me!

She loves me!—And I have grown in stature in my own eyes,—I can tell you this, you who understand such things—I worship myself, ever since she loves me!

Is this presumption, or a feeling for the way things truly are?—I can think of no man who represents a threat to me in Lotte's heart. And yet, whenever she speaks of her intended, speaks of him with such warmth and love, I feel as if I had been stripped of all honour and rank and had my sword taken from me.

16 July

Ah, how the thrill of it shoots through me if my finger happens to touch hers or our feet meet beneath the table! I recoil as if from a fire, yet some secret force draws me on again—and all my senses grow dizzy.—And oh! her innocence and her ingenuous spirit do not feel what agonies these little intimacies put me through. Indeed, if she places her hand on mine when we are talking and, excited by the conversation, moves closer, so that her divine breath brushes my lips—I feel as if I shall sink into the ground, as if I had been struck by lightning.—But still, Wilhelm, if I should ever dare abuse this heaven, and her trust!—You know what I mean. No, my heart is not so corrupt! Weak, yes, quite weak enough!—And is that not in fact corruption?—

She is sacred to me. All my desires are stilled in her presence. I never know what I am about when I am with her; it is as if my very soul were throbbing in every nerve.—There is a melody, a simple but moving air, which she plays on the piano, with angelic skill. It is her very favourite tune, and the moment she plays the first note I feel delivered of all my pain, confusion and brooding fancies.

Every word they say about the magical power of ancient music strikes me as plausible. How that simple song enthrals me! And how well she knows when to play it, often at times when I would gladly put a bullet through my head! The darkness and madness of my soul are dispelled, and I breathe more freely again.

18 July

What is the world to our hearts without love, dear Wilhelm? What is a magic-lantern without light? You have only to position the lamp and there you have the most colourful pictures on your white wall! And even if there were nothing more to it all than that, a few fleeting shadows, it would still give us happiness to stand there like young children, delighted by the marvellous apparitions. Today I was unable to visit Lotte because I had an engagement I could not cancel. What could I do? I sent my servant to her house, so that I would at least have someone about me who had been near her today. How impatiently I awaited his return! and how I rejoiced on seeing him again! I should have liked to take hold of his head and kiss him, but I was too embarrassed.

They say that if Bologna barite is placed in sunlight it absorbs the rays and will glow for a while in the dark. It was exactly like that with me and this fellow. The thought that her eyes had rested on his face, his cheeks, the buttons of his tunic and the collar of his *surtout* endeared those things to me endlessly, and made them sacred! I would not have parted with the lad for a thousand thalers at that moment. I felt so happy in his presence.—God forbid that you should laugh at this, dear Wilhelm. Are they nothing but shadows and apparitions if we are happy?

19 July

'I shall see her today!' I exclaim in the mornings when I rise and look up to the beautiful sun with a glad heart; 'I shall see her today!' And then I have no other wishes all day long. Everything, everything is included in that one hope.

20 July

I cannot quite warm to your suggestion that I accompany the ambassador to——. I am no great friend of subordination; and we all know that, what is more, he is a disagreeable person. You say that my mother would like to see me kept occupied, which made me laugh. As if I were not occupied now; and does it make much fundamental difference whether I count peas or lentils? The affairs of the world are no more than so much trickery, and a man who toils for money or honour or whatever else in deference to the wishes of others, rather than because his own desire or needs lead him to do so, will always be a fool.

24 July

Since you are so concerned that I should not neglect my drawing, I would prefer to say nothing at all about the question than to admit how little I have done of late.

I have never felt happier, and my feelings for Nature, down to tiny pebbles and blades of grass, have never been so full and acute, and yet—I do not know how to express myself; my imaginative powers are so weak, and everything slides and shifts before my soul, so that I cannot grasp the outlines; but I fancy I might make a go of it if I had some clay or wax to model. If things are like this much longer I really shall get some clay and model it, even if all I produce is dumplings!

I have started on a portrait of Lotte three times, and three times I have failed disgracefully; which depresses me all the more since I could take a very good likeness not so long ago. So then I cut a silhouette profile[28] of her, and that will have to do.

26 July

Yes, dear Lotte, I shall arrange and order everything; give me as many things to do as you like, and as often as possible. One thing, though: if

I might ask you not to use sand to dry the notes you write me . . . ? Today I raised it hastily to my lips, and was left a gritty crunching in my teeth.

26 July

I have often determined not to see her so frequently. But who could abide by such a decision? Every day I give in to the temptation, and take my sacred oath that I shall stay away on the morrow. And once the next day comes I hit upon some irresistible reason again, and in no time at all I am at her side. The evening before she may have said: 'You will come tomorrow, won't you?'—And who could stay away then? Or she gives me some errand to run, and I think it proper to take her the answer myself; or else it is a fine day and I walk to Wahlheim, and once I am there it is only another half an hour to Lotte's!—I am too close to her magic realm—snap your fingers! and there I am. My grandmother used to tell a story about a magnetic mountain: ships that sailed too close were suddenly stripped of all their ironwork, the nails flew to the mountain and the wretched travellers perished in the falling timbers.

30 July

Albert has arrived, and I shall leave; even if he were the best and noblest of men, one to whom I should be willing to think myself inferior in every respect, it would be unbearable to see him before me, in possession of such perfections.—Possession!—Enough, dear Wilhelm; her intended is here! A dear and honest man whom one cannot help liking. Fortunately I was not present when she welcomed him home! It would have broken my heart. He is so considerate, too, and has not yet kissed Lotte a single time in my presence. May God reward him for it! I have to love him for the respectful way he treats the girl. He is well disposed towards me, which I take to be Lotte's doing rather than his own feeling; for in such matters women have a delicate sense of tact, and quite rightly so, because if they can keep two admirers on good terms with each other, however rarely it might be possible, the advantage is always their own.

And anyway, I cannot help esteeming Albert. His tranquil evenness of manner is in marked contrast to the turbulence of my own disposition, which I cannot hide. He is a man of feeling, and knows very well what Lotte is worth. He seems to be almost free of ill-humour, which as you know is the human evil I loathe above all others.

He considers me a man of some sensitivity; and his own triumph is augmented by my attachment to Lotte, and the joyful warmth her every action produces in me, and he loves her all the more. I cannot tell whether he does not sometimes pester her with petty jealousies; if I were in his position, I should not be entirely safe from that demon jealousy.

But be that as it may, I can no longer take pleasure in being with Lotte. What shall I call it?—Folly, or delusion?—Why give it a name? The thing speaks for itself!—Everything I now know I knew before Albert's arrival; I knew I had no claim on her, nor did I raise any—That is to say, as far as it is possible not to have one's desires in the presence of so much loveliness—So now the wretched dolt stands there gaping, the moment his rival really does come back and takes his girl away.

I grind my teeth and mock my own misery; though I would heap infinite mockery on anyone who said I should be resigned since there was no alternative.—Get these idiotic pip-squeaks off my back!—I go rambling in the woods, and if my walk takes me to Lotte's and I find Albert sitting in the summerhouse with her in the greenery, and I cannot bear it any more, I behave like a complete fool, and clown about, and talk gibberish.—'For God's sake,' Lotte said to me today, 'please spare us scenes like last night's! When you're so merry you are terrifying.'—Between you and me, I keep a careful watch for times when he is busy elsewhere; and whoosh! there I am, and I'm always happy to find her on her own.

For goodness' sake, dear Wilhelm, I did not mean you when I complained that people who urge us to be resigned to inevitable fate are unbearable. It truly did not enter my head that you might be of such an opinion. Basically you are right, of course. But, dear friend, with this one proviso: things in this world seldom come down to an either-or decision, and possible courses of action, and feelings, are as infinitely various as kinds of noses on the gamut from hooked to snub.

Forgive me, then, if I concede your entire argument and still try to find a loophole between the either and the or.

You say that I can either hope to win Lotte or give up my hopes. Very well; in the former case, try to press on and attain the fulfilment of your wishes, and, in the latter, pull yourself together and try to shake off miserable emotions that can only wear your powers away. —Dear friend, well said!—but how easily it is said.

Would you insist that some wretch whose life is slowly but surely being drained away by lingering disease put an end to his miseries with one sharp thrust of his dagger? Does not the malady that consumes his strength also rob him of the courage to seek his deliverance?

True, you might counter with a similar analogy: who would not rather have his arm amputated than risk his life by doubt and hesitation?—I do not know!—Let us not bother with analogies. Enough.—Wilhelm, I have moments of courage when I could leap to my feet and shrug it all off, moments when—if I only knew where to go—I should be on my way.

The same evening

Today I happened upon my diary, which I have been neglecting for some time, and I am astounded to see how I went ahead in all this, step by step, in full awareness of what I was doing! How clearly I saw my position, and yet how childishly I behaved; and I still see it clearly now, and yet there is no sign of improvement.

10 August

I could be living the best and happiest of lives if only I were not a fool. It is not easy to find the agreeable circumstances that gladden Man's soul all together, as I have done here. Ah, one thing is sure: the heart alone is the source of our happiness.—To be a member of that delightful family, to be loved like a son by the old man, like a father by the children, and by Lotte!—and then Albert, an honest soul who never disturbs my happiness with any unpleasant ill-humour; who embraces me in a spirit of heartiest friendship; and who loves me better than anyone else on earth, Lotte excepted!—It is a delight, dear Wilhelm, to hear us talking about Lotte when we are out walking together; nothing on earth is more ludicrous than our connection, and yet I often have tears in my eyes.

When he tells me about her excellent mother,[29] and how on her deathbed she commended her house and children into Lotte's keeping and Lotte herself into Albert's care, and how ever since Lotte has been alive with a quite different spirit, concerned for their welfare and conscientious about being a true mother, never allowing a moment to pass without showing love or turning her hand to some work, yet never losing her cheerfulness and lightheartedness—I walk by his side, picking flowers by the wayside, and carefully arrange them in a bouquet—then toss them into a stream we pass, and watch as they are gently borne away.—I do not know if I wrote that Albert will be remaining here and is to have a well-salaried position at court, where he is very popular. I have rarely come across anyone to equal his orderliness and diligence in business affairs.

12 August

No doubt about it, Albert is the best fellow on earth. Yesterday the two of us had a remarkable scene. I called on him to take my leave, for I was in the mood for riding out into the hills, which is where I am writing from now. As I was pacing up and down his room I noticed his pistols.—'Lend me your pistols,' I said, 'for my journey.'—'By all means,' said he, 'if you will take the trouble to load them. I only have them there *pro forma*.'—I took one of them down, and he continued: 'My caution backfired on me quite nastily, and ever since I have wanted nothing to do with such things.'—I was curious to hear the story.—'For a good three months,' he told me, 'I was staying in the country at a friend's, and I had a brace of pistols with me, which I kept unloaded, and slept well. Then one rainy afternoon when I was sitting about doing nothing, for some reason it occurred to me that we might be attacked, we might need the pistols, we might—you know how it is.—I gave them to the servant to clean and load; and he was fooling about with the maid, trying to scare her, when (God knows how) the gun went off, with the ramrod still in the barrel, and shot the rod straight through the girl's right hand, smashing her thumb. So I got all the weeping and wailing, and had the doctor's bill to pay as well, and since then I have kept all my guns unloaded. My dear chap, what use is caution? We cannot anticipate every possible danger. But still . . .'—Now you well know that I like the man dearly, but I draw the line at his *but still*; after all, can we not take it for granted that every general rule has its exceptions? But he is so scrupulous! And if he thinks he has made some over-hasty or generalized or half-true statement he will not stop offering you qualifications and amend-ments and riders, till in the end the substance of what he has said has disappeared. On this occasion he preached a veritable sermon, and finally I ceased to listen to him, fell to brooding and suddenly placed the mouth of the pistol against my forehead, above my right eye.—'What rot!' said Albert, taking the pistol from me. 'What are you playing at?'—'It isn't loaded,' I said.—'Even if it isn't,' he retorted impatiently, 'what are you up to? I cannot imagine how a man can be so foolish as to shoot himself; I find the mere thought repellent.'

'Why is it,' I demanded, 'that when people speak of things they must promptly pronounce them foolish or clever, or wicked or good! Whatever does it all mean? Have you really grasped the true and inmost nature of an action? Can you really give a definite account of the reasons why it happened, and why it had to happen? If you understood them, you might not judge so hastily.'

'But you will grant that certain actions are wrongful,' said Albert, 'no matter what their motives.'

I shrugged, and conceded the point.—'And yet, my dear friend,' I went on, 'there are exceptions to that rule too. True, it is wrong to steal: but if a man goes thieving to save himself and his family from starvation, are we to pity him or punish him? Who will first cast a stone[30] if a husband sacrifices his unfaithful wife and her worthless seducer in the heat of his righteous wrath? or if a girl abandons herself for one joyful hour to the irresistible pleasures of love? Even our laws, cold-blooded and pedantic as they are, are moved to relent and forgo punishment.'

'That is entirely different,' answered Albert, 'because a man wholly under the influence of his passions has lost his ability to think rationally, and is regarded as intoxicated or insane.'

'Ah, you sensible people!' I cried, with a smile. 'Passions! Intoxication! Insanity! You are so calm and collected, so indifferent, you respectable people, tut-tutting about drunkenness and holding unreasonable behaviour in contempt, passing by like the priest and thanking God like the Pharisee[31] that you are not as other men. I have been intoxicated more than once, my passions have never been far off insanity, and I have no regrets: because I have come to realize, in my own way, that people have always felt a need to decry the extraordinary men who accomplish great things, things that seemed impossible, as intoxicated and insane. How intolerable it is in everyday life, too, to hear them say, the moment anyone does something remotely free or noble or out of the ordinary, "The fellow's drunk, he's off his head!" You should be ashamed of yourselves, you sensible people, you sages!'

'These are your usual fanciful thoughts,' said Albert; 'you exaggerate everything, and in this case at least you are certainly wrong to compare suicide, which is what we were talking about, with great accomplishments, since it cannot be considered as anything but a weakness. After all, it is easier to die than to endure a harrowing life with fortitude.'

I was on the point of breaking off our conversation; for no argument so throws me as when somebody trots out a meaningless platitude when I am speaking straight from the heart. However, I controlled myself, since I had often heard the comment and had still more often been annoyed at it, and rejoined with some warmth: 'You call it weakness? Beware of being deceived by appearances. If a

61

nation is groaning under the unendurable yoke of a tyrant, is it weakness to rebel at last and shatter the chains? If a man, shocked to find his house on fire, senses his strength is heightened, so that he can easily carry some burden he could barely lift in calmer moments—or if a man is so enraged by an insult that he takes on six opponents and overcomes them—would you call them weak? Well, my good friend, if such exertions are to be seen as strength, why should the greatest of endeavours be thought the opposite?'—Albert considered me, and remarked: 'Pray pardon me, but the examples you mention seem to have no bearing on what we are discussing.'—'That may well be,' said I. 'People have often accused me of having an incoherent way of arguing. But let us see if there is any other way of imagining the state of mind of a man who resolves to throw off this burden of life, a burden which is so pleasant as a rule. We may only speak of a matter, after all, if we have felt it. Human nature,' I went on, 'has its limits, and can take joys, sorrows and pain up to a certain point, but is annihilated once the threshold is crossed. The question, therefore, is not whether a man is weak or strong, but whether he can endure the full extent of his sufferings, be they of a moral or physical nature. And in my opinion it would be as misconceived to call a man cowardly for taking his own life as it would be to say a man who dies of a malignant fever was a coward.'

'What paradoxical absurdities!' exclaimed Albert.—'Not as paradoxical as you might suppose,' I replied. 'You concede that if a disease so severely attacks our constitution as to wear away or suspend our powers of resistance, so that we cannot recover of our own accord or regain our normal way of life through some happy counter-attack, we call it a sickness unto death.[32] Let us now apply this to the spirit, my dear friend. Consider a man confined within his bounds, influenced by impressions, beset by ideas, till one day a growing passion overthrows his contemplative composure and destroys him. It is all in vain if a calm and sensible man grasps the condition of this unfortunate, all in vain if he advises him! Just as it would be vain for a healthy man standing by a sickbed to want to impart even the slightest part of his own strength to the invalid.'

Albert found this all too general. I reminded him of a girl who had been found drowned in the river[33] not long ago, and told him her story once again.—'She was a good young creature who had grown up in the narrow environment of household tasks and a weekly routine of work. She had no greater pleasures to look forward to than to dress up on a Sunday in the finery she'd gradually managed to buy and go for a stroll around town with her friends, or perhaps, on special feast-days, to go dancing, and the rest of the time to spend some lively and warm-hearted hour chatting with a neighbour about the causes of some quarrel or the motives behind some ill-intentioned gossip.—At length her fiery nature sensed deep-seated needs, which the flatteries of men made more urgent; bit by bit she lost her taste for her former pleasures, until one day she met a man to whom she was irresistibly attracted and for whom she felt unfamiliar feelings, and so she attached all her hopes to him, forgot the world about her, heard and saw and felt nothing but him, her one and only, and was consumed with longing for her one and only. Her one and only's pleasures were the empty ones of inconstant vanity, but none the less all her wishes aimed at being his, and finding in an everlasting union with him all of the happiness she lacked, all of the joys she longed for. He made repeated promises that assured the certainty of her hopes, and the bold caresses that inflamed her desires quite overpowered her soul. She floated in a barely conscious, dreamlike state, anticipating every conceivable joy, tensed with the utmost excitement, and finally stretched out her arms to embrace the fulfilment of all her wishes—and her lover deserted her.—Stunned, insensible, she totters on the brink of the abyss. All is darkness around her, she understands nothing, she has no hope, no consolation! He has deserted her, he who made her feel alive. She can see neither the wide world before her nor the many others who could compensate for her loss. She feels alone, forsaken by the whole world—and, driven to despair by the terrible suffering in her heart, she plunges blindly into the depths, to drown her torment in the great embrace of Death.—That, you see, is the story of many a mortal, dear Albert! And now tell me if it is not a case of sickness? Nature cannot find the way out of the labyrinth, where all a soul's powers are confused and at odds, and the poor mortal must die. Woe to anyone who can look on and say, "The foolish girl! If only she had waited, and let time heal, her despair would have passed and she would have found someone else to comfort her."—One might as well say, "The fool, to die of a fever! If only he had waited till he recovered his strength, his fluids[34] were improved and his blood was calmer: it would all have been well, and he would still be alive today!"'

Albert, who could still not see the point of comparison, made some more objections, one of them being that I had only spoken of an ignorant girl; but he was unable to grasp how a man of sense, who was not so limited and had a broader perspective, might be excused. —'My friend,' I cried, 'human kind is merely human, and that jot of rational sense a man may possess is of little or no avail once passion is raging and the bounds of human nature are hemming him in. Quite the contrary—but more of that another time . . .' So saying, I picked up my hat. Oh, my heart was full to bursting—And we parted without either having understood the other. But then, it is never easy for men to understand each other in this world.

15 August

Without doubt, the only thing that makes Man's life on earth essential and necessary is love. I sense that Lotte would be sorry to lose me, and the children can only ever imagine me coming again on the morrow. Today I went there to tune Lotte's piano, but was unable to do so because the little ones kept on at me to tell them a story, and Lotte herself said I should do as they wished. I cut the bread for their supper, which they are now almost as glad to have from me as from Lotte, and told them the episode about the princess waited on by hands [35] I learn a great deal in the process, I assure you, and I am astonished at the impressions the stories make on them. Sometimes I have to invent a detail, which I then forget in the second telling, whereupon they instantly tell me it was different the time before; so that I now try to recite my tales off pat in a singsong tone, without any changes. It has taught me that when an author writes a second, revised version of his story it must needs be bad for the book, however great the poetic improvement. The first impression finds us ready enough, and Man is so constituted as to swallow the most bizarrely improbable things; but that impression sticks, and woe to him who would erase or obliterate it!

Did it really have to be like this?—that the source of Man's contentment becomes the source of his misery?

My heart's immense and ardent feeling for living Nature, which
overwhelmed me with so great a joy and made the world about me a
very paradise, has now become an unbearable torment, a demon that
goes with me everywhere, torturing me. At other times, when I gazed
from the crags across the river to those hilltops yonder, taking in the
entire fertile valley and seeing all about me burgeoning and putting
forth new life; when I saw the mountains, clad from foot to peak with
thick and mighty trees, and the winding valleys shaded by the most
delightful woods, and the river flowing gently amongst the whispering reeds and mirroring the lovely clouds which a soft evening breeze
wafted across the heavens; and when I heard the birds carolling in the
forest all around, and millions of midges danced their giddy dance in
the last red glow of sunlight, and a last setting ray brought forth the
humming beetle from its grassy retreat, and all the busy buzzing
made me study the ground, where the moss that gains its sustenance
from the unyielding rocks, and the heath that grows on the barren
sand, revealed to me the inmost, sacred warmth of the life of
Nature—at such times, how ardently my heart embraced it all: I felt
as if I had been made a god in that overwhelming abundance, and the
glorious forms of infinite Creation moved in my soul, giving it life.
Immense mountains surrounded me, chasms yawned at my feet,
streams swollen by rain tumbled headlong, rivers flowed below me
and the forests and mountains resounded; and I could see those
immeasurable and incomprehensible powers at work in the depths of
the earth, and above the earth's surface, beneath the heavens, there
teemed all the infinite species of Creation. Everything, all of it, is
peopled with myriad forms; and then mankind comes building its
nests, crowding together safely in little houses, and supposes it rules
over the whole wide world! Poor fool! imagining everything to be so
small, because you are yourself so small.—From the most inaccess-
ible of mountains, to the desert where no man has ever set foot, to the
very ends of the unknown ocean, breathes the spirit of the eternal
Creator, rejoicing in every speck of dust that is alive and knows

Him.—Ah, how often in former times did I long for the wings of a crane that passed overhead, to fly to the shores of the measureless sea, and there drink the full joy of Life from the foaming goblet of the Eternal, and taste, if only for a single moment, with the limited power that is in my breast, one drop of the blessed serenity of that Being who makes all things, in Himself and through Himself.

Dear brother, only the recollection of those times gives me any pleasure. Even the effort of recalling those inexpressible feelings and uttering them once more uplifts my soul, and then leaves me doubly aware of the fearfulness of the condition I am now in.

It is as if a curtain had been drawn from before my soul, and this scene of infinite life had been transformed before my eyes into the abyss of the grave, forever open wide. Can you say that anything *is*, when in fact it is all transient? and all passes by as fast as any storm, seldom enduring in the full force of existence, but ah! torn away by the torrent, submerged beneath the waves and dashed against the rocks? There is not one moment that does not wear you away, and those who are close to you, nor any one moment when you yourself are not a destroyer, of necessity: the most innocent of walks costs thousands of wretched grubs their lives, one step wrecks what the ant laboriously built and treads a little world into an ignominious grave underfoot. Ha! It is not the major but rare catastrophes of the world, the floods that wash away your villages, the earthquakes that swallow up your cities, that move me; what wastes my heart away is the corrosive power that lies concealed in the natural universe—in Nature, which has brought forth nothing that does not destroy both its neighbour and itself. And so I go my fearful way betwixt heaven and earth and all their active forces; and all I can see is a monster, forever devouring, regurgitating, chewing and gorging.

21 August

In vain I stretch out my arms to her when morning comes and I gradually waken from deep dreams, in vain I look for her in my bed at night when some happy, innocent reverie has tricked me into believing I was sitting with her in a meadow, holding her hand and covering it with a thousand kisses. Ah, still half asleep I reach for her, cheered to think she is there—and a flood of tears pours from my sorely beset heart, and I weep inconsolably over my sombre future.

22 August

It is quite disastrous, Wilhelm: all my active energies have been cast down into restless listlessness, and I can neither be idle nor accomplish anything. My imagination has deserted me, my feeling for Nature is gone, and books nauseate me. Once we are lost unto ourselves, everything else is lost to us. I swear there are times when I wish I could be a day labourer, simply in order to have something to look forward to in the day ahead, a sense of purpose, hope. I often envy Albert when I see him up to the ears in paperwork, and fancy I should be content if I were in his position! I have repeatedly been on the point of writing to you and the minister, applying for the embassy appointment which you assure me I would obtain. I too believe I would do so; the minister has a long-standing regard for me, and has often urged me to devote myself to some business; and for one brief hour I am on the brink of going ahead. But then, when I consider it anew, and the story of the horse that grew weary of freedom, had itself saddled and bridled, and was ridden into the ground[36] occurs to me—I do not know what to do.—What is more, dear friend! may not my yearning for change be a restless impatience within me, which will pursue me everywhere?

28 August

It is true that if my sickness could be cured, these people would cure me. Today is my birthday,[37] and early in the morning a package arrived from Albert. When I opened it, the first thing I set eyes on was one of the pink ribbons[38] Lotte was wearing when I met her, which I had often asked her for since then. The package contained two duodecimo volumes, the little Wetstein Homer,[39] an edition I had frequently wished for, to save me hauling Ernesti's about on my walks. There you have it!—How they anticipate my wishes, how they grant friendship's little attentions, which are worth a thousand times more than breathtaking presents that merely prove the giver's vanity and humiliate us. I have been kissing that bow a thousand times over, and with every breath I take the memory of those few happy, irrecoverable days returns to me. Do not suppose I am complaining, Wilhelm, but, say what you like, life's blossoms are but an illusion! How many pass away without leaving a trace behind, how few of them bring forth fruit, and how few of those fruits grow ripe! And nevertheless there are still enough; and yet—oh, dearest brother! —can we be capable of neglecting ripened fruits, despising them, and leaving them to rot?

Farewell! It is a glorious summer; I often sit up in the fruit trees in Lotte's orchard, using a pole to get at the pears on the topmost branches. She stands below and takes them as I pass them down.

30 August

Wretched being! What a fool you are! Are you not deceiving yourself? What is the point of this wild and ceaseless passion? I can no longer pray except to her; my imagination beholds no figure but hers; and I see the things of the world about me only in relation to her. And as a result I do enjoy many a happy hour—until I have to tear myself away from her again! Ah, Wilhelm! the things my heart compels me to!—When I have been with her for two or three hours, entranced by her ways and the divine expressiveness of her words, and my senses gradually become excited, my sight grows dim, I can hardly hear a thing, I have difficulty breathing, as if a murderer had me by the throat, and then my heart beats wildly, trying to relieve my tormented senses and only making their confusion worse—Often, Wilhelm, I do not know if I exist at all! And if melancholy is not allowed to prevail, and Lotte does not permit me the miserable solace of weeping on her hand for relief, I have to leave, and go out—and then I wander far and wide in the fields, and take pleasure in climbing a precipitous mountain, and beating a path through thick forest, hurt by the briers, torn by the thorns! Then I feel somewhat better! Somewhat! At times I am so tired and thirsty that I lie out on the ground, late at night with the full moon high above me, or I rest on a crooked tree trunk in the remote depths of the forest, to ease my sore feet a little, and in my exhaustion I slumber peacefully in the first light of day. Oh, Wilhelm! My soul is so beset that I long for the pampered ease of a hermit's isolated cell, for a hair-shirt and a barbed scourge. Adieu! I see no end to my misery but the grave.

3 September

I must leave! Thank you, Wilhelm, for stiffening my wavering resolve. This last fortnight I have been thinking of leaving her. I must go. She is in town again, with a friend. And Albert—and—I must go!

10 September[40]

What a night that was! Now, Wilhelm, I can endure anything. I shall never see her again! Oh, why can I not fall at your breast, dear friend, and tell you, with a thousand tears and raptures, of the emotions that are belaying my heart. Here I sit, gasping for air, trying to compose myself, waiting for daybreak; I have ordered the horses for sunrise.

Ah, she will be sleeping peacefully, without a suspicion that she will never see me again. I have torn myself away; and I had the fortitude not to betray my intention during a two-hour talk. And, my God, what a talk it was!

Albert had promised that he and Lotte would be in the garden immediately after supper. I stood on the terrace under the tall chestnut trees, watching for the last time as the sun set on that delightful valley and gently flowing river. I had stood there so often with her, and had watched that glorious spectacle, and now—I strolled up and down the avenue I loved so dearly. Some secret sympathy had often drawn me there before I knew Lotte, and at the beginning of our friendship we were pleased to discover our mutual liking for the spot, which truly is one of the most romantic ever created by the gardener's art.

First there is an extensive view between the chestnut trees—ah, I seem to remember I have already described it at length in an earlier letter: the tall beeches that hem one in, the nearby thicket that makes the avenue duskier, and then at last an enclosed little square which offers all the thrills of solitude. I can still sense the feeling of foreboding it gave me when I stood there for the first time one bright midday; some gentle intuition told me it was to be the setting for scenes of blissfulness and pain.

I had been indulging for about half an hour in the sweet and soulful thought of farewell and returning when I heard them ascending to the terrace. I ran to meet them, caught hold of her hand with a tremble and kissed it. We had just emerged on to the terrace when the moon rose above the wooded hill; we spoke of various things, and, without noticing it, approached the melancholy summerhouse. Lotte stepped inside and sat down, Albert sat beside her, and so did I; but I was too agitated to sit for long; I got to my feet, stood before her, paced to and fro, sat down again; I was in a fearful state. She drew our attention to the beautiful effect of the moonlight, which was illuminating the entire terrace beyond the beech trees: a glorious sight, which was rendered all the more striking by the deep gloom which enclosed us on all sides. We remained silent, and after a while she observed: 'I can never ever go walking in the moonlight without the thought of my dear departed ones coming to my mind, or without being filled with a sense of death and what lies in the future. There will be a life for us after death, Werther!' she went on, her voice full of the most exalted emotion; 'but will we find each other again? and know each other? What do you suppose? What do you say?'

'Lotte,' I said, giving her my hand, my eyes filling with tears, 'we shall see each other again! We shall meet again, both here and in the hereafter!'—I was unable to continue—Did she have to put that

70

question, Wilhelm, with my heart burdened with the dreadful parting to come!

'What of our dear departed ones,' she went on: 'do they know how we are? Can they sense when things go well with us, can they feel that we remember them with fond love? Oh, the figure of my mother is always by me when I sit amidst her children in the silent evening hours, amidst my children, and they crowd about me as they used to crowd about her. Then I shed a tear of longing, and raise my eyes to heaven, and wish she could look down for one moment and see that I am keeping the promise I made at the hour of her death: to be a mother to her children. With what emotion I then cry out: "Dear mother, forgive me if I cannot be to them what you were! Ah, I do everything I can, they are clothed and fed, and ah! more than that, they are cared for and loved. If only, dear sainted mother, you could behold our harmony, you would glorify God, with the most ardent of gratitude, for answering your last and tearful prayers for the well-being of your children." '—

Those were her words! But oh, Wilhelm, who can repeat what she said! How can these cold, dead words on the page convey the divine flowering of her spirit? Albert interrupted her gently: 'It affects you too deeply, dear Lotte! I know your soul likes to dwell on these ideas, but I beseech you . . .'—'Oh, Albert,' she said, 'I know you cannot forget those evenings when papa was away, the little ones had been put to bed, and the three of us sat at the little round table. You would have a good book but rarely got round to reading anything—The company of that noble soul was preferable to everything, was it not? That beautiful, gentle, cheerful, eternally busy woman! God knows the tears I have shed in my bed, imploring Him to make me her equal.'

'Lotte!' I exclaimed, falling at her feet, seizing her hand and shedding a thousand tears on it—'Lotte! God's blessing and the spirit of your mother are upon you!'—'If only you had known her,' she said, squeezing my hand;—'she was worthy of being known by you!'—I thought it would be the end of me. Nobody had ever paid me a greater or prouder compliment. She continued: 'And this woman was doomed to perish in her prime, when her youngest son was not yet six months old! It was a short illness; she was calm and resigned, though it grieved her to part from her children, particularly the little one. When her end was approaching she said, "Bring the children to

71

me." I led them in, the young ones who did not know what was happening and the elder ones who were numb with pain, and they stood by her bed; and she raised her hands and prayed for them, kissed them in turn and sent them out, and then said to me: "Be a mother to them."—I gave her my hand.—"Dear daughter," she said, "what you are promising is a great deal. It is the heart of a mother and the eye of a mother. I could often tell from your grateful tears that you felt what that means. Show a mother's care to your brothers and sisters, and be as faithful and obedient to your father as a wife. You will be a comfort to him."—She asked for him, but he had gone out, to conceal from us his intolerable anguish; the poor man was shattered. You were in the room, Albert. She heard somebody moving about, asked who it was, and desired you to go to her; and that look of contentment and peace she gave you and me, knowing we would be happy, happy together . . .'—Albert fell at her breast and kissed her, exclaiming: 'We are happy! And we will be in future!' —Albert had completely lost his usual composure, and I was quite beside myself.

'And this woman, Werther,' she resumed, 'was taken from us! Dear God! to think that one can see what one holds dearest in life borne away. Nobody feels it more acutely than the children; for a long time they kept on complaining that the black men had carried away their mama!'

She stood up, and I, both moved and devastated, remained seated, holding her hand.—'It is time we were going,' she said.—She tried to withdraw her hand, but I held it more tightly.—'We shall see each other again,' I cried. 'We shall find each other, we shall pick each other out from among the many. I am going,' I continued, 'going of my own free will, yet if I thought we were parting for ever I could not bear it. Farewell, Lotte! Farewell, Albert! We shall meet again.' —'Tomorrow, I expect,' she countered in jest.—How I felt that 'tomorrow'! Ah, she little knew, as she withdrew her hand from mine—They left the avenue, and I stood watching them in the moonlight, threw myself on the ground and wept my heart out, then leapt to my feet and ran out on to the terrace, from where, down below in the shade of the tall linden trees, I could still make out the white gleam of her dress as she walked to the garden gate—and I stretched out my arms—and she vanished.

⟨ BOOK TWO ⟩

20 October

We arrived here yesterday. The ambassador[41] is indisposed and will therefore be staying indoors for a few days. If only he were not so morose, all would be well. I can see all too clearly that Fate has severe trials in store for me. But courage! A lighthearted spirit can put up with anything. A light heart? It makes me laugh, the way the words flow from my pen: oh, if there were a little more lightheartedness in my veins I should be the happiest creature under the sun. Am I to despair of my own powers, my own gifts, when others with paltry abilities and talents go showing off, smugly self-satisfied? Dear God who bestowed all these gifts on me, why didst Thou not keep half back, and in their place grant me confidence and contentment?

Patience! Patience! All will improve. And I tell you, my dear fellow, you were right. I feel far better within myself now that I am among these people, kept busy day in, day out, watching their doings and goings-on. It is true that, since we are so constituted as to be forever comparing ourselves with others and our surroundings with ourselves, our happiness or misery depends on the things in our environment; and, this being so, nothing is more dangerous than solitude. It is in the nature of our imagination to be rising, impelled and nurtured by the fantastic images of poetry; and it conceives of a chain of beings with ourselves as the most inferior and everything else more glorious and with greater perfections. All of this is quite natural. We often feel that we lack something, and seem to see that very quality in someone else, promptly attributing all our own qualities to him too, and a kind of ideal contentment as well. And so the happy mortal is a model of complete perfection—which we have ourselves created.

On the other hand, once we set to work diligently, in spite of all our shortcomings and the toilsomeness of it, we quite often find that in our leisurely, tacking style we make better headway than others who sail and row—and it gives us a genuine sense of ourselves, to keep pace with others or indeed outstrip them.

26 November

I am beginning to find things quite tolerable here, on the whole. Best of all is that I am kept well occupied; and these many and various people, all the new characters, provide my soul with a colourful spectacle. I have struck up an acquaintance with Count C.,[42] whom I esteem more highly every day, a man of great learning and mature judgement but by no means cold, thanks to his broad understanding; in his company I feel that he is very sensitive to friendship and love. I had some affair to transact with him once, and he took an interest in me on perceiving, from my first words, that we understood each other, and that he could converse with me in a way he could not converse with everyone. I cannot sufficiently praise the kindly openness with which he behaves towards me. There is no truer, warmer pleasure in this world than to behold a great soul opening up towards oneself.

24 December

The ambassador is extremely trying, as I foresaw. He is the most punctilious oaf imaginable, doing everything step by step, meticulous as a maiden aunt, a man whom it is impossible to satisfy because he is never satisfied with himself. I like to get on with my work, and once it is finished that is that; but he is perfectly capable of returning papers to me and saying: 'That is fine, but have another look through it, one can always find a better word or an apter particle.'—At such times I could clean take leave of my senses. Not a single and or conjunction may be omitted, and he is a sworn enemy of all the inversions[43] of syntax that sometimes occur to me; if a sentence is not played to a familiar tune he cannot understand a word of it. Being associated with such a person is a woeful business.

My close acquaintance with Count C. is the only compensation. Recently he quite frankly told me how dissatisfied he was with the slowness and laboriousness of my ambassador. 'People make things more difficult for themselves and for others too. Still,' he said, 'one must be resigned to it, like a traveller who has to cross a mountain; naturally his route would be a deal more comfortable, and shorter, if the mountain were not there, but, as it is, he has to get on with climbing it!'—

My old fellow is well aware of the count's preference for myself over him, and it annoys him, so that he seizes every opportunity to speak ill of the count to me, whereupon I naturally reply in his defence, which only makes things worse. Yesterday he really vexed me by aiming a remark at me as well: he observed that the count handled the affairs of the world quite well, got on with his work, and wrote presentably, but he had as little solid learning as all geniuses. With that he looked at me with an expression that seemed to ask, 'Did that one go home?' But it did not produce the desired effect in me; I despised the man for thinking and behaving in such a way. I stood up to him, and countered with considerable warmth. The count, I said, was a man deserving of respect, for his character and for his knowledge. 'I have never met anyone,' I said, 'who has succeeded so well in broadening the horizons of his spirit, and extending his knowledge in countless areas, and still turning his hand to the affairs of everyday life.'—This was too much for his poor brain, and I took my leave, so as not to be put in a temper by some further nonsense.

And it is all your fault, for talking me into this yoke and singing the praises of a busy life! If the man who grows potatoes and goes to town to sell his corn is not better employed than I am, let me slave away ten whole years longer in the galleys I am chained in now.

And this glittering misery, the tedium of these awful people cooped up together here! and their greed for rank, and the way they are forever watchful and alert for gain or precedence: the most wretched and abominable of passions, quite nakedly displayed. There is one woman, for instance, who tells everyone who will listen about her family and estate, so that a stranger would needs think her a fool with

75

an inflated opinion of her drop of aristocratic blood and of the importance of her estate.—But the fact of it is much worse: this same female is no more than a clerk's daughter from this neighbourhood. —I cannot grasp how humankind can be witless enough to debase themselves so utterly.

I am, however, growing daily more aware how foolish it is to judge others by one's own standards, dear friend. And since I give myself enough trouble as it is, and this heart of mine is so turbulent—ah, I am glad to let others go their own ways. If only they would allow me to do the same.

What provokes me worst of all are our fateful bourgeois distinctions of rank. Of course I know as well as anyone that differences of class are necessary, and that they work greatly to my own advantage: but I wish they would not place obstacles in my way when I might enjoy a little pleasure, some scrap of happiness in this world. When I was out walking recently I got to know a Miss von B.,[44] an amiable creature who has retained a very natural manner amidst this inflexible life. We took such pleasure in our conversation that when we parted I asked permission to call on her. She granted the request so readily that I could hardly wait for a fitting time to visit her. She does not come from here, and is living with an aunt. The old lady's physiognomy[45] was off-putting. I paid a great deal of attention to her and addressed most of my conversation to her, and in less than half an hour I could see for myself what the young lady afterwards admitted to me herself: that her dear aunt has been left lacking everything in her old age, and has no presentable fortune or wits, no source of strength other than her pedigree, no protection but that sense of class in which she has barricaded herself, and no pleasure apart from looking down on middle-class citizens from the heights of an upper-storey window. She was supposedly a beauty in her youth, but trifled away her life, first by tormenting many a poor youth with her caprice, and then in riper years owing obedience to an old officer who, in exchange for that obedience and a tolerable sum, agreed to spend the Brazen Age[46] with her, and then died. Now, in her Iron Age, she is alone, and no one would pay her the smallest respect if her niece were not so amiable.

8 January 1772

What people these are, whose entire souls are occupied with protocol and ceremony, who devote their devious creative energies, for years on end, to moving one place higher up at table! It is not as if they had no other affairs to see to: quite the contrary, the work piles up because they are so busy with petty, irksome questions of advancement that they have no time for important matters. Last week at a sledging excursion a quarrel flared up and everybody's fun was quite spoilt.

What fools they are not to see that the position one occupies is in reality immaterial, and that he who is in the topmost position so rarely plays the most important role! Many a king is ruled by his minister, many a minister by his secretary! And which of them is in first position? As I see it, the one whose vision takes them all in and who has the power or cunning to harness their energies and passions to the execution of his own plans.

20 January

I have to write to you, my dear Lotte, from the parlour of this humble country inn where I have taken refuge from a dreadful storm. As long as I was in D., that miserable hole, living among strangers who were alien to my heart, I never had time, not a single moment, when my heart might have prompted me to write to you; and now in this cottage, isolated and confined, with snow and hail beating against the little window, my thoughts turned to you first of all. The minute I entered, your figure appeared before me, and the memory of you, oh Lotte! so sacred, so warm! Dear God! it is a first moment of happiness once again.

If you could but see me, my dear friend, amidst that whirl of trivial amusements! My senses are quite dried out! There is not a single instant when the heart is full, not one single hour of bliss! nothing! nothing!—It is as if I were watching a raree-show, seeing the little men and horses moving about, and often I wonder if it is not an optical illusion. I play the game myself, or rather I am played with, like a puppet, and from time to time I grasp my neighbour's wooden hand and withdraw with a shudder. In the evenings I resolve to enjoy the next day's sunrise, but I cannot quit my bed; during the daytime I look forward to the delights of moonlight, and then I stay in my room. I do not quite know why I rise or why I go to bed.

There is no sour dough in my life to set it working and rising; I have lost the delights that kept my spirits up in the depths of night, and the charms that awoke me in the mornings are gone.

I have met only one female creature here, one Miss von B., who resembles you, my dear Lotte, if it is possible to resemble you. 'Look at this!' I hear you say: 'The fellow has taken to paying pretty compliments!' Which is not totally false. I have been on my best behaviour for some time, since there is no alternative, and am very witty, and the ladies say no one praises them as nicely as I do (nor tells such lies, you must add, since the one is not possible without the other, if you understand what I mean). But I was meaning to tell you of Miss von B. She has a great soul, which gazes straight at one from her blue eyes. Her rank is a burden and satisfies none of the wishes of her heart. She is longing to put all this brouhaha behind her, and we spend many an hour imagining country scenes of unadulterated bliss; and then, ah! we speak of you! Often she has to pay homage to you, or rather she does not have to, she does so of her own volition, likes to hear me speak of you, and loves you.—

Oh, if only I were sitting at your feet in that dear, familiar little room, with the dear little ones romping about me; if they were too loud for your liking I would gather them round me and keep them quiet with some frightful fairy-tale.

The sun is setting gloriously on a landscape glittering with snow, the storm has passed, and I—I must return and be locked in my cage once more.—Adieu! Is Albert with you? And what—? God forgive these questions!

8 February

For a week we have had the most awful weather, and I find it is most welcome. For as long as I have been here not one single beautiful day has dawned but someone has spoilt or soured it for me. So if it is rainy or windy or frosty or wet from a thaw, I think: ha! it can be no worse at home than if I were out and about, and vice versa; and I am content. When the sun rises in the morning and heralds a fine day, I can never resist exclaiming: there they have another gift of the gods which they can ruin for each other! There is nothing at all they do not spoil. Their health, their reputation, their happiness, their leisure! Generally they do it out of stupidity, incomprehension and narrow-mindedness, and if you can believe what they say it is always with the best of intentions. At times I could go down on my knees and beg them not to do such reckless damage to their own hearts.

17 February

I fear that my ambassador and I will not be able to endure each other much longer. The man is totally intolerable. His style of working and going about his affairs is so ridiculous that I cannot help contradicting him, and often I deal with something in my own way and in accordance with my own judgement, and then, needless to say, he never approves. Recently he complained at court about this, and the minister reprimanded me: gently, it is true, but none the less he reprimanded me, and I was on the point of resigning when I received a private letter* from him, a letter I submitted to on bended knee and with reverence for its exalted, noble spirit of wisdom. I respect the way he rebukes my hypersensitivity, and pays tribute to my excessive notions of diligence, influence on others and perseverance

* Out of deference to this excellent gentleman it has been thought best to remove the letter referred to, and another which is mentioned at a later point, from this edition; since it was not felt that the public's warm gratitude could excuse taking the audacious liberty of publication.

in business affairs, which he describes as the plucky ambition of youth, saying he does not wish to destroy it but merely to moderate it and divert it into areas where it can be put to proper use and produce its rightful powerful effect. So now I have the strength for another week, and have regained my inner composure. Tranquillity of the soul is wonderful, as is joyful peace of mind. If only, dear friend, these precious treasures, beautiful and priceless as they are, were not so fragile too.

20 February[47]

God bless you, my dear friends, and may He grant you all those happy hours He takes from me!

I am grateful to you, Albert, for deceiving me: I was waiting for news of your wedding date, and had decided to take down Lotte's silhouette profile from my wall on that day, with all solemnity, and bury it amidst my other papers. So now you are married, and her picture is still there! Well, so be it. And why not? I know that I am still with you, that your position is unaffected, dear Albert, by my place in Lotte's heart, that indeed I hold second place in her heart, and wish to keep it, must keep it. Oh, it would drive me insane if she could forget—Albert, the very thought is hell. Albert, farewell! Farewell, thou angel of heaven! Farewell, Lotte!

15 March

This latest adversity will drive me away from here. I grind my teeth!—The devil take it! There is nothing I can do about it, and all of you are to blame who urged and goaded and tormented me to take a position I had no taste for. Now I have what was coming to me! and so do you! And just so that you will not go telling me yet again that it is my own extreme ideas that spoil it all, let me tell you, my dear sir, a plain tale, as pretty as any chronicler could write it.

80

As you know, as I have told you a hundred times already, Count C. is fond of me and accords me special favour. I dined with him yesterday, the very day when the ladies and gentlemen of the nobility regularly assemble at his house in the evening; it never crossed my mind, nor did it occur to me that we subordinates do not belong in that company. I dined with the count, and afterwards we walked up and down the great hall in conversation, together with Colonel B., who joined us, and the time for the assembly gradually approached. God knows it never entered my head. Then in came the most gracious Lady von S., with her spouse and her scheming little goose of a flat-chested, trimly corseted daughter, and in passing they gave me looks and twitched their nostrils in their usual, oh-so-aristocratic way; and, since I cannot abide this breed, I was about to take my leave, and was just waiting for the count to disengage himself from their appalling twaddle when my Miss von B. entered the hall. My heart always feels freer the moment I see her, so I stayed, stationed myself behind her chair, and did not notice until some time had passed that she was speaking less openly than normally and with a certain embarrassment. It was striking. Can she too be like the rest of them? I wondered, vexed, and was on the point of going, but nevertheless I remained, because I did not believe it of her, would have liked to see her innocent of the charge, and was still hoping for some kind word from her—you may see it as you wish. The hall had filled meanwhile. There was Baron F. in all the attire he wore to the coronation of Franz I;[48] Privy Councillor R., who is addressed in company as Mr von R., with his deaf wife, etc.; not forgetting J., wretchedly turned out, his old-fashioned Franconian garb patched up with modern rags: all of them were gathered there, and I passed the time of day with one or two I knew, though they were very brief in their replies. I was busy with my own thoughts, and only paid attention to my Miss von B. I did not register that the women were whispering at the far end of the hall, that the whispering was spreading to the men, or that Mrs von S. was speaking to the count (Miss von B. told me all this afterwards), until at length the count approached me and took me aside in the bay of a window—'You know how absurd things are,' he said. 'I gather the company takes exception to your presence here. I should not wish on any account—' 'Your Excellency,' I interrupted, 'I beg a thousand pardons; I should have thought of it sooner, but I

81

trust you will forgive the oversight; I had intended to take my leave some time ago, but my wicked demon prevented me,' I added, smiling and bowing.—The count shook my hand feelingly, in a manner that spoke volumes. I made my inconspicuous disappearance from the illustrious assembly and left, took a two-wheeler, and drove out to M. to stand on the hill and watch the sun set and read that magnificent book in Homer where Odysseus enjoys the hospitality of the excellent swineherd.[49] Which was all very pleasant.

That evening I returned to supper; there were still a few people in the parlour, who had turned back the tablecloth and were playing dice on a corner of the table. Then Adelin, a worthy fellow, came in, laid down his hat on seeing me and, coming over to me, said softly: 'You have had a trying experience, I gather.'—'Me?' said I.—'The count turned you out of the assembly.'—'The devil take them!' said I; 'I was glad to be out in the fresh air.'—'So much the better,' said he, 'that you can take it so lightly. I confess it distresses me; it is already all over town.'—At this point the business first began to upset me. Whenever anyone came and sat at the table and looked at me, I thought he was looking at me because of it! Which made for bad feelings.

So today I am offered sympathy wherever I go, and I hear that those who envy me are triumphantly saying that there you have it, that is what becomes of cocky people who are arrogant on account of their bit of brain and imagine they can disregard conventional form, and whatever other rubbish they blether—and I could plunge a knife into my heart. Say what you please about independence of spirit; I defy you to show me the man who can endure hearing scoundrels gabbing about him when they have some advantage over him; ah, it is only when their prating is without foundation that one can easily ignore them.

16 March

Everything is conspiring against me. Today I met Miss von B. in the avenue, and could not resist talking to her and, as soon as we were some distance from her company, indicating how deeply her recent behaviour had affected me.—'Oh, Werther,' she said, in a tone of fervent emotion, 'surely you who know my heart could not interpret my distress in such a way? How I suffered on your account, from the very second I entered the hall! I saw it all coming, and a hundred times I was on the point of telling you. I knew that von S. and T. and their menfolk would rather leave than remain in your company, and I knew the count has to stay in favour with them.—And now all this talk!'—'What can you mean, dear miss?' I asked, trying to conceal my alarm; for everything Adelin had told me the day before yesterday boiled in my blood at that moment.—'How much it has already cost me!' said the sweet creature, with tears in her eyes.—I could no longer control myself, and might have thrown myself at her feet at any moment.—'Explain what you mean!' I cried.—The tears coursed down her cheeks. I was beside myself. She dried her tears, without attempting to hide them.—'You know my aunt,' she began; 'she was present, and oh! what a light she sees it in! Dear Werther, last night and this morning I had to endure a sermon concerning my acquaintance with you, and I have been obliged to hear you condemned and disparaged, and I was neither able nor permitted to say much in your defence.'

Every word she said was like a dagger in my heart. She did not sense what a mercy it would have been to keep all of it from me, and she went on to predict the gossip that was still to come, and described the kind of person that would relish the triumph, and how they would be tickled by the comeuppance my arrogance, and the deprecatory view of others which I have long been accused of, had brought me, and how they would rejoice. To hear all of this from her, dear Wilhelm, in a tone of the sincerest sympathy!—I felt annihilated, and am still in a rage within. I wish someone would have the courage to mock me to my face, so that I might thrust my sword through his body; the sight of blood might afford me some relief. Ah, I have snatched up a knife a hundred times, meaning to relieve my sorely beset heart. People tell of a noble breed of horses that instinctively bite open a vein when they are exhausted and feverish, in order to breathe more freely. I often feel the same, and am tempted to open a vein and so find eternal freedom.

24 March

I have tendered my resignation to the court, and hope it will be accepted; you must forgive me for not having first asked your consent, but it has become imperative that I leave, and I know everything you would say to persuade me to stay, so—Break the news gently to my mother; there is nothing I can do about it, and she will needs be resigned to my being unable to ease the shock for her either. Of course it is bound to hurt her. To see her son's admirable career to the office of privy councillor and then ambassador so rudely interrupted, and her son marching back to the stables with the other animals! Well, make of it what you will, and analyse the possible conditions under which I could or should have stayed; the fact of it is that I am leaving, and, so that you know where I am moving to, the Prince of —— is here, and takes great pleasure in my company; and, having heard of my intention, he has asked me to spend the spring on his estate with him. I am to be left entirely to my own devices, he promises, and, since we see eye to eye on all matters barring one, I intended to trust to fortune and go with him.

19 April

Thank you for your two letters. I did not reply because I was leaving this letter open until the court accepted my resignation; I was afraid my mother might approach the minister and make it difficult for me to do as I intended. But now it is done, my discharge has been granted. I cannot tell you how reluctantly it was given, or what the minister wrote to me—you would only begin your lamentations over again. The crown prince has sent me a parting present of twenty-five ducats, with a note that moved me to tears; so I shall not be needing the money I recently asked my mother for.

5 May

I leave here tomorrow, and, since the place of my birth is only six miles out of my way, I plan to visit it again and recall those long-gone days of happy dreams. I shall enter by the very gate my mother and I left by when she quit that dear, familiar place after the death of my father and locked herself away in her unbearable city. Adieu, Wilhelm; you will be hearing about my expedition.

9 May

I made my pilgrimage to my home parts with all the reverence of a true pilgrim, and was moved by a number of unanticipated feelings. I had the carriage stop by the great linden tree, a quarter of an hour's walk from the town on the road to S., and got down, telling my postilion to drive on, so that on foot I might let my heart dwell on all the freshness and vividness of every recollection. So there I stood beneath the linden, which in my boyhood served as both the goal and the limit of my walks. How things have changed! In those days, blissfully ignorant, I longed to go out in the unknown world, where I hoped my heart would find the sustenance and pleasure to meet and satisfy the ambitions and desires that were in my breast. And now I was returning from that wide world—and oh! my friend, how many of my hopes had gone awry, how many of my plans had been destroyed!—Spread out before me I saw the mountains which a thousand times over had been the object of my wishes. I could sit here for hours on end, longing to be over there, my inmost soul rejoicing in the woods and valleys which looked so pleasantly dusky; and if I then had to return home at a fixed time, how loth I was to leave that charming spot!—I approached the town, saluting all the old, familiar bowers in the gardens and disliking the new ones, and disliking all the other changes that had been made as well. I entered by the gate, and immediately felt quite at home. My dear fellow, I shall not give you a detailed account; delightful as it was for me, the telling could not be

85

anything but dull. I had decided to lodge on the market square, next to our old house. On my way there I noticed that the schoolroom, where that honest old woman herded us children into the fold, had become a shop. All the restlessness and tears, the heaviness of heart and the mortal fear I endured in that hole came back to me.—Every step I took offered new revelations. No pilgrim in the Holy Land encounters as many places of sacred memory, nor can his soul very well be as devoutly moved as mine.—Let me give you just one example. I followed the river downstream to a farm I knew, a walk I always liked to take, to the spots where we used to see how many times we could bounce flat stones off the water when we were lads. I remembered so clearly how I would stand there gazing at the flowing water, following it with my head full of romantic notions, imagining the exciting parts it would pass through, and all too soon finding my imagination failed me; yet the water flowed on, and so did my imagination, till I was quite lost in the contemplation of an invisible distance.—That, my dear fellow, is how our ancestral fathers were: their lives as limited and yet as happy, their feelings and poetry with that quality of childishness! When Odysseus speaks of the measureless sea and the boundless earth, it is all so true and human, so inwardly and closely felt, and so mysterious. What use is it if I, like any schoolboy, can now parrot that the earth is round? Man needs only a small patch of earth for his pleasures, and a smaller one still to rest beneath.

Now I am at the prince's hunting lodge. He is a true and simple soul with whom one can live very pleasantly. There are odd people about him, though, whom I do not understand. They do not seem to be rogues, but neither do they strike me as honest people. At times they seem honest, and still I cannot bring myself to trust them. I am sorry to hear the prince often speaking of things he has merely heard tell of, or read about; when he does so, he adopts the point of view of the one who presented the matter to him.

I am also disturbed to find he values my mind and abilities more highly than my heart, which is my only source of pride, and indeed of everything, all my strength and happiness and misery. The things I know, anyone can know—but my heart is mine and mine alone.

25 May

I had a plan I was meaning to tell you nothing about until I had carried it out: now that it has fallen through I may as well mention it. I was going to become a soldier; it has been my heart's desire for a long time. That was the main reason why I accompanied the prince here, since he is a general in the service of ——. When we were out walking together I spoke to him of my intention; he advised me against it, and I should have had to be in the grip not of a mere whim but of a regular passion to have disregarded his reasons.

11 June

Say what you please, I cannot stay here any longer. What am I to do here? Time hangs heavy on my hands. The prince is generosity itself to me, and yet this is not where I belong. Basically we have nothing in common. He is a man of the intellect, but his intellect is of a very ordinary quality; I take no greater pleasure in his company than in reading a well-written book. I shall remain another week and then start on my wanderings once more. The best thing I have accomplished here is my drawings. The prince has a feeling for art, and would feel all the more directly if he were not fettered by dreadful scholarly approaches and the usual terminology. At times I grind my teeth with impatience when I am expatiating to him on Nature and art, with the full ardour of my imagination, and he suddenly supposes he is making a valuable contribution if he interjects some learnedly coined label.

16 June

Indeed, I am nothing but a wanderer and a pilgrim on this earth! And what more are you?

18 June

Where I am going? I shall tell you, in confidence. I have to remain here a fortnight longer after all, and then I have fooled myself into thinking I shall visit the mines at ——; but essentially that is not true, I only want to be near to Lotte again, that is all. And I laugh at this heart of mine—and do as it dictates.

29 July

No, it is well! it is all well!—I—her husband! Oh dear God who created me, if Thou hadst bestowed that happiness on me, my entire life would have been one unceasing prayer. But I am not disputing Thy wisdom; forgive these tears, forgive my vain wishes!—She my wife! If I might only have held the dearest creature under the sun in my arms—It sends a tremble through my whole body, Wilhelm, when Albert takes her by her slender waist.

And—dare I say it? Why not, dear Wilhelm? She would have been happier with me than with him! Oh, he is not the man to satisfy all the wishes of her heart. He lacks a certain sensitivity, he lacks—well, make of it what you will. His heart does not beat in unison with hers when—oh!—when they read a passage in a favourite book where my heart and Lotte's beat together; there were a hundred other instances when we expressed our feelings concerning the behaviour of some third person and found they coincided. My dear Wilhelm!—He loves her with his entire soul, no doubt, and love of that order deserves a great deal!—

I have been interrupted by an unbearable visitor. My tears are dry. I do not quite have my wits about me. Adieu, my dear fellow!

4 August

I am not the only unfortunate. All men are disappointed in their hopes and cheated out of their expectations. I visited the good young woman under the lindens. The eldest boy ran towards me, and his shout of joy brought his mother to us, looking extremely despondent. The first thing she said was: 'Ah, dear sir, my poor Hans died!' —Hans was the youngest of her boys. I was silent.—'And my husband,' she said, 'has returned from Switzerland without the inheritance, and if it had not been for the help of some good people he would have had to beg his way home; he fell ill with a fever on the way.'—There was nothing I could say, but I gave the little one a present; she asked me to accept a few apples, and I did so and then left the place, which was filled with sad memories.

21 August

At a moment's notice my mood changes. Sometimes it seems a happy prospect of life is becoming visible to me, but ah! for a mere instant!—When I am lost in my daydreams I cannot help wondering: what if Albert were to die?—You would!—yes, and she would—and then I fantasize till I am at the brink of the abyss, and I flinch back with a shudder.

When I go out by the gateway, taking the road I drove along that first time I picked up Lotte for the ball, how very different it all is! It is all over, all of it! There is not a hint of the world that once was, not one pulse-beat of those past emotions. I feel like a ghost returning to the burnt-out ruins of the castle he built in his prime as a prince, which he adorned with magnificent splendours and then, on his deathbed but full of hope, left to his beloved son.

3 September

At times I cannot grasp that she can love another man, that she dare love another man, when I love her and her alone with such passion and devotion, and neither know nor have anything but her!

4 September

Yes, that is how it is. As Nature's year declines into autumn, it is becoming autumn within me, and all about me. My leaves are yellowing, and already the leaves of the nearby trees have fallen. Didn't I write to you once, when I was first here, about a farmer lad? I have now inquired after him again in Wahlheim; they say he has been expelled from service and nobody wants any more to do with him. Yesterday I met him quite by chance, on the road to a nearby village, and spoke to him, whereupon he told me his story, one which moved me deeply, as you will readily understand once I repeat it to you. And yet, why bother? Why should I not keep the things that trouble and grieve me to myself? Why should I depress your spirits too? Why should I go on providing you opportunities to pity and berate me? No matter; all of this must be my fate as well!

At first the man answered my questions with a quiet sadness which seemed to indicate a reticent disposition; but, as if he had recognized both me and himself once again, he quickly made more open confession of his errors, and lamented his misfortune. If only, my friend, I could submit his every word to your judgement! He admitted, indeed he told me with a kind of relish, taking pleasure in the recollection, that his passion for his mistress had increased day by day until in the end he did not know what he was about or (as he put it) what was to become of him. He was unable to eat or drink or sleep, he forever had a lump in his throat, he did things he ought not to have done, he forgot the orders he had been given, it was as if some wicked demon were after him: till one day when he knew she was in an upstairs room he followed her, or rather was drawn after her. She would not listen to his entreaties, so he tried to take her by force. He told me he did not know what had got into him, and called God to witness that his intentions towards her had always been honourable and that he had had no more cherished desire than to marry her, and spend his life with her. By this time he had been talking for a while, and began to hesitate, like one who still has something to say but lacks the courage to say it; till at length he confessed to me, somewhat abashed, that she had permitted him certain little intimacies, and had allowed him to be very close to her. Two or three times he broke off, assuring me repeatedly and in the liveliest of tones that he was not saying it to make her seem a bad woman (as he put it), that he loved and esteemed her as much as he ever had, that he had never uttered a word of this to anyone else and that he was only telling me in order to convince me that he was not a wicked or unreasonable man.—At this point, dear friend, I sing my old familiar tune, as I always will: if only I could show you the man as he stood before me, as he still stands before me! If only I could tell it as it ought to be told, you would feel why I sympathize with his fate, and why I am compelled to do so! But enough; since you know my own fate as well, and know me, you will understand well enough what draws me to unfortunates in general, and to this unfortunate in particular.

On reading this letter over again I see I have forgotten to tell you how the story ended, though you could easily imagine it for yourself. She fended him off; her brother, who had hated him for a long time and had long wished him out of the house, for fear that if his sister remarried his own children would lose their inheritance, which promises a handsome future as long as she is childless—her brother came hurrying in, and instantly kicked the lad out of the house, and talked so much about the affair that the woman could not have taken the lad back in even if she had wanted to. I gather she now has a new servant, who is likewise a bone of contention between her and her brother; and the lad tells me people say she is sure to marry him; but he is determined not to see it happen.

What I have been telling you is not exaggerated or in any way embroidered, and indeed I might say I have told it feebly, feebly, and have dragged it down by using the prim and proper words society always uses.

His love, his constancy and his passion are no poetic fabrication.

This love really exists, most purely amongst that class of people we call uneducated and uncouth. We are educated—and our education has rendered us good for nothing! I beseech you, read his story carefully. Today, in setting it down, I have my composure; you can see from my writing; I am not scrawling and blotting as I normally do. Read it, my beloved friend, and bear in mind that it is also the tale of your humble servant. Yes, that is how things have been with me, and how they will be, and I am not half as worthy or resolute as this poor unfortunate, with whom I scarcely dare compare myself.

5 September

She had written a note to her husband, who was in the country attending to some business. It began: 'My dearest love, come home as soon as you can. I am filled with joy at the thought of your return.'—A friend who stopped by brought word that for a number of reasons Albert would not be returning so soon. The note was left lying there and that evening I chanced upon it. I read it and smiled; she asked what I was smiling at.—'What a divine gift imagination is,' I exclaimed; 'for one moment I tricked myself into thinking it was addressed to me.'—She broke off what she was doing and looked displeased, and I was silent.

6 September

It cost me a wrench but in the end I decided not to wear the simple blue frock-coat I had on when I first danced with Lotte any more; it had become quite unpresentable. Still, I have had a new one made, exactly like the other, down to the collar and lapels, and the very same buff waistcoat and breeches as well.[50]

But it does not feel quite right. I do not know—I suppose in time I shall grow to like it better.

12 September

She has been away for a few days, collecting Albert. Today I entered her parlour and she came to meet me, and I kissed her hand, overcome with joy.

A canary flew off the mirror and perched on her shoulder.—'A new friend,' she said, coaxing it onto her hand, 'which I got for the children. Isn't he a dear? Look at him! If I give him some bread he flutters his wings and pecks oh-so-daintily. He kisses me too: watch!'

She held the little creature to her mouth and lovingly pressed it to her sweet lips, as if it were capable of feeling the bliss it was enjoying.

'He shall kiss you too,' she said, and held the bird towards me.—Its little beak moved from her mouth to mine, and when it touched me with a peck it was like a breath of love, a promise of pleasure to come.

'His kiss,' I said, 'is not wholly free of a desire; he wants food, and these empty endearments leave him dissatisfied.'

'He will eat out of my mouth, too,' she said.—She offered it a few crumbs on her lips, and smiled with all the joyful happiness of innocent and loving fellow-feeling.

I averted my gaze. She ought not to do it, ought not to excite my imagination with these scenes of divine innocence and bliss, or awaken my heart from that sleep which the indifference of life lulls it to!—And why not?—She has such trust in me! and knows how much I love her!

15 September

It could drive me crazy, Wilhelm, to think there are people devoid of appreciation or feeling for that little which has real value on earth. You remember the walnut trees under which I sat with the worthy vicar of S. and Lotte, those magnificent walnut trees which, as God is my witness, always filled my soul with the greatest joy! How cosy they made the vicarage courtyard, and how cool! And how glorious their

spreading branches were! and our recollections of the worthy ministers who planted them many years ago. The schoolmaster often told
us the name of one of them, having heard it from his own grandfather;
he must have been an excellent man, and his memory was sacred to
me whenever I stood beneath those trees. I assure you, Wilhelm, that
yesterday, when our talk turned to them, there were tears in the
schoolmaster's eyes when he told me they had been cut down. Cut
down! The thought of it drives me out of my mind, and I could gladly
murder the villain who struck the first blow. And I must stand by, I
who would go into mourning if I had two such trees in my own yard
and one of them died of old age. But I take some consolation, my
dearest friend, in seeing the nature of human feeling. The whole
village is upset, and I hope the vicar's wife will soon realize, once the
butter and eggs and other signs of favour stop, what a wound she has
inflicted on the place. For it was she who did it, the wife of the new
incumbent (our old vicar having passed on too), a lean, sickly creature
with good reason to care little for the world, since no one cares much
for her. She is a fool who affects to be learned,[51] occupies herself with
studying the canonical books of the Bible, works hard on today's
new-fangled moral and critical reformation of Christianity and
shrugs off Lavater's rhapsodic effusions; her health is quite ruined,
and so she takes no delight in God's earth. Only a creature such as
this could have been capable of cutting down my walnut trees. As you
see, Wilhelm, I cannot recover from the shock. Imagine it: the falling
leaves made her courtyard dank and dirty, the trees obstructed her
daylight, and when the nuts were ripe the lads threw stones at them,
which got on her nerves and disturbed her profound thoughts when
she was weighing the relative merits of Kennicot, Semler and
Michaelis.[52] On seeing the people in the village so upset, especially
the old ones, I said: 'Why did you stand by and let it happen?'—'In
these parts,' they told me, 'there's nothing you can do if it's the
steward's orders.'—But one thing served them right. The steward
and the vicar, who normally does not profit in any way from his wife's
silly notions but thought this time he stood to gain, intended to divide
the timber between them; but the revenue office heard of it and told
them to hand it over. They still had an old claim to that part of the
vicarage grounds where the trees stood; and the timber was sold to
the highest bidder. So they have been laid low! Oh, if only I were a

prince! I would have the vicar's wife, and the steward, and the revenue office—A prince!—If I really were a prince, I should have better things to concern me than the trees in my dominion!

10 October

Simply to see her dark eyes restores my spirits! And what distresses me, Wilhelm, is that Albert does not seem as happy as—he hoped —or as I—should have expected to be—if—I do not care for all these dashes, but there is no other way I can express this—and I imagine this is clear enough.

12 October

Ossian[53] has ousted Homer from my heart. What a world that exalted soul leads me into! To wander across the heath in the pale moonlight, with the gale howling and the spirits of his forefathers in the vaporous mists! To hear amidst the roar of a forest torrent the faint moans of the spirits in their mountainside caves, and the laments of that mortally stricken maiden weeping over the four mossy, grassed-over stones that mark the grave of the noble warrior who was her lover! And then to find him, that grey-haired bard, wandering on the vast heath, seeking the places his forefathers knew, and then, ah! finding their tombstones, and raising his eyes in lament to the sweet star of evening as it sinks in the waves of the rolling sea! And times gone by are relived in the hero's soul, times when the warm rays of the sun lighted the brave the way to danger and the moon shone on their triumphant ship returning fresh from victory! And I read the deep sorrow in his brow, and see that last exalted soul tottering deserted and exhausted to the grave, deriving new and painful joy from the insubstantial presence of the shade of his departed loved one; and I see him look down at the cold earth and the tall grasses waving in the

95

wind and cry out: 'Tomorrow the traveller shall come,—he shall come, who beheld me in beauty, and he shall ask: "Where is the singer, where is he, the excellent son of Fingal?" His eye shall seek me in the field around, but he shall seek me in vain on earth.'[54]—Oh, my friend! I wish that I might draw my sword, like some noble warrior, and deliver my prince from the painful torments of a long drawn-out death, and send my soul to go with the demi-god I had set free.

19 October

Ah, this void! this terrible void I feel in my breast!—I often think that if only I could hold her to my heart for once, just once, that void would be entirely filled.

26 October

Yes indeed, I am certain, my dear fellow, and grow more certain all the time, that the existence of any single creature is of little, very little importance. One of Lotte's friends called on her, and I withdrew to the next room to fetch a book, was unable to read, and took up my pen to write. I could hear them talking in low tones; they were telling each other the unimportant news and gossip of the town, who was marrying whom, who was ill, very ill.—'She has a dry cough, her face has become terribly bony and she keeps fainting; I wouldn't give a kreutzer for her chances,' said the visitor.—'N.N. is in a very bad state too,' said Lotte.—'He already has swellings,' said the other. —In my imagination, vivid as it is, I was at the bedside of these poor people, and saw them turning their backs upon life with such reluctance, and—Wilhelm! the ladies were chatting about it as indifferently as if it were the death of a stranger.—And if I now gaze around me, at this room, with Lotte's dresses about me, and Albert's papers, and the furniture I am so familiar with, down to this very ink-pot, and think: see how much you mean to this household now! Everything. Your friends value you! You often make them happy, and your heart in turn feels it could not do without them; and yet—if you were to go, if you were to depart from this intimate circle, would they feel the void, how long would they feel the void that your loss tore open in their fate?—how long?—Oh, Man is so transient a being that even where his existence is most secure, even where his presence makes its sole true impression felt, he must fade and disappear from the memories and souls of his loved ones, soon, oh so soon!

27 October

I could often tear my heart open and beat my poor head on seeing how little people can mean to each other. If I do not offer love and joy, happiness and warmth, ah! the other will not bring them to me either; nor will my heart, overflowing with rapture, move him at all if he is cold and listless.

The same evening

I have so much, and my feelings for her absorb it all; I have so much, and without her it is all nothing.

30 October

I have already been on the point of falling at her breast a hundred times! Dear God in heaven knows how it feels to behold so much loveliness before one and not be allowed to embrace it; and, after all, that embrace is the most natural of Man's instincts. Do not children reach out for everything that attracts them?—Then why should not I?

3 November

God knows I often retire to my bed wishing (at times even hoping) that I might never wake up: and in the mornings I open my eyes, see the sun once again, and am miserable. Oh, if only I could follow some mood and blame the weather, or a third person, or failure in some enterprise; then the intolerable burden of my discontent would trouble me half as much. Woe! I feel all too clearly that the blame lies solely with me—No, not the blame!—It is enough that the source of my wretchedness lies within myself, as the source of all my joy once did. Am I not still the very same man who once walked in an excess of happiness, paradise before him at every step, with a heart that could embrace the whole world in the fullness of love? And now that heart is dead and no longer gives me joy, my eyes are dry, and my senses are not refreshed by heartfelt tears any more but furrow my brow with fearful worries. I suffer a great deal because I have lost the sole pleasure in my life, that sacred and inspiring power to create new worlds about me;—it is gone! When I gaze from my window at the distant hills and see the morning sun breaking through the mist above them and shining upon the tranquil meadows, and the river gently meandering amongst the leafless willows—oh! all the glories of Nature are frozen to my eye, like a varnished painting, and all the delights are powerless to extract one drop of joy from my heart to refresh my mind, and there I stand, in the sight of God, like a dried-up spring, like a broken pitcher.[55] I have often prostrated myself on the ground and prayed to God for tears, like a farmer praying for rain when the heaven over his head is brass[56] and the earth is parched.

But ah! I sense that God does not send rain or sunshine in response to our importunate pleas; and the reason why those times whose recollection so torments me now were so blissful was that I awaited His spirit with patience, and received the joys he bestowed upon me with a full and deeply grateful heart.

98

She has reproached me for my excesses!—though in the most amiable of ways. My excesses consist in going on to empty the bottle when on occasion I drink a glass of wine.—'Do not do it!' she said; 'think of Lotte!'—'Do you need to tell me to think of you!' said I. 'Think of you!—I do not think of you; you are always before my soul. Today I was sitting at that spot where you recently alighted from the carriage . . .'—She changed the subject to prevent me from pursuing it any further. My friend, I am lost! She can do with me whatever she pleases.

15 November

Thank you, Wilhelm, for your heartfelt sympathy and well-meant advice. I beg you not to be too concerned; let me endure it; for all my fatigue of spirit, I still have the strength to see it through. I value religion, as you know, and feel that it affords support to the weary and solace to the afflicted. But can it, or need it, do so for all men? If you consider this wide world you will see thousands for whom religion has not done so, thousands for whom it will not do so, whether they have it preached to them or not; need it offer comfort to me, then? Does not the Son of God say Himself that no man can come unto him, except it were given unto him of His Father?[57] What if it be not given unto me? What if the Father means to keep me, as my heart tells me?—I beg you not to misinterpret this; I am revealing my entire soul to you; otherwise I should prefer to have remained silent on the subject, as indeed I am reluctant to speak on matters of which I know no more than anyone else. What is the Fate of Man, but to suffer his appointed due and drink the cup of bitterness?—and if the Son of Man prayed that the cup pass from him,[58] why should I show off and pretend it tastes not bitter but sweet? And why should I feel ashamed in that dreadful moment when my entire self trembles on the edge of being and not-being,[59] and the past flashes upon the dark abyss of the future like lightning, and all about me disintegrates, and the world goes to its doom with me? At such a time, is it not the voice of a creature utterly beset, with no inner resources left, and plunging to inexorable destruction, that groans in the inmost depths of its insufficient powers: 'My God, my God, why hast thou forsaken me?'[60] And should I feel ashamed to say it? Should I be afraid of that moment, when even He was afraid who stretcheth out the heavens like a curtain?[61]

21 November

She does not see or feel that she is concocting a poison that will be my destruction and her own; and in ecstasy I drain the goblet she offers me and which spells my downfall. What is the meaning of the kindly look with which she often—often?—no, not often, but sometimes gazes at me? or of the sweetness of temper with which she receives my involuntary outbreaks of feeling? or of the sympathy for my sorrows that I see in her expression?

As I was leaving yesterday she offered me her hand and said: 'Adieu, dear Werther!'—Dear Werther! It was the first time she ever called me dear, and it went right through me. I have said it over to myself a hundred times, and last night as I was about to go to bed and was talking all manner of stuff to myself I suddenly said: 'Good night, dear Werther!' and then could not help laughing at myself.

22 November

I cannot pray: 'Leave her to my keeping,' and yet it often seems as if she were mine. I cannot pray: 'Give her to me,' for she belongs to another man. I play witty games with my own pain; and, if I indulged myself in the sport, could compose an entire litany of antitheses.

100

She senses what I am enduring. Today her gaze pierced my very heart. I found her alone; I said nothing, and she looked at me. And I no longer saw in her that gentle beauty, or the light of a great spirit; in my eyes, it had all vanished, and the vision that moved me, that gaze she turned upon me, was a more glorious one, full of the deepest compassion and the sweetest sympathy. Why could I not throw myself at her feet? and fall at her breast, and respond with a thousand kisses? She retreated to the piano and accompanied her playing with harmonious sounds breathed forth in a sweet and tender voice. Her lips had never looked so lovely; it was as if they opened thirstily to drink in the sweet tones that streamed from the instrument, and what was returned from her pure mouth was merely a secret echo—if only I could describe it to you!—I resisted no longer, bent forward, and vowed: Never shall I dare implant a kiss on these lips where the spirits of heaven dwell.—And yet—I want to—Ha! You see, it is like a barrier my soul has come up against—such bliss—and then doomed to expiate the sin. Sin?

26 November

At times I say to myself: your fate is unique; consider other mortals as happy—none has ever been as tormented as you.—Then I read the work of an ancient poet and it is as if I were contemplating my own heart. I have so much to endure! Ah, have ever men before me been so miserable?

30 November

It seems I am really not destined to recover my wits! Wherever I go I encounter something to drive me to distraction. And today! oh, the Fate of Man!

I was walking by the water at midday, lacking any appetite for lunch. It was all dreary, and a cold, wet westerly wind was blowing from off the mountains, and grey rain clouds were gathering over the valley. From a distance I made out a fellow in a worn, green coat scrabbling about the rocks, apparently looking for herbs. As I came nearer he turned at the sound of my approach, and I beheld a most interesting physiognomy, features dominated by silent sadness but otherwise expressive of a good and honest nature; he had pinned up his black hair in two ringlets, and the rest was plaited into a thick tail which hung down his back. Since his attire suggested he was a man of the lower orders, I assumed he would not take it amiss if I took an interest in what he was doing, and so I asked him what he was looking for.—'I am looking for flowers,' he answered, with a deep sigh, 'but I cannot find any.'—'Well, it isn't the season for them,' I said with a smile.—'There are so many flowers,' he said, climbing down to me. 'I have two kinds in my garden, roses and honeysuckle, one of them was given to me by my father, they grow like weeds; I have been searching for two days but cannot find them. There are always flowers out there, yellow ones and blue ones and red ones, and centaury has a very pretty bloom. I can't find any of them.'—His face was twisted by an odd, twitchy smile. 'Strictly between ourselves,' he said, placing a finger to his lips, 'I promised my sweetheart a bunch of flowers.'—'And very nice too,' said I.—'Oh, she has a lot of other things,' he said. 'She's rich.'—'But she will still value your posy,' I replied.—'Oh, she has jewels,' he went on, 'and a crown.'—'And what is her name?'—'If only the general estates[62] would pay me,' he added, 'I should be a new man! Yes, there was a time when I was very contented! Now it is all over. Now I am . . .' His eyes filled with tears and he raised them expressively towards heaven.—'And you were happy then?' I asked.—'Ah, if only I could be happy again!' he said. 'I was thoroughly in my element, contented and cheerful and light-hearted.'—'Heinrich!' called out an old woman who was coming along the path; 'Heinrich, where are you hiding? We have been looking for you everywhere. Come in to lunch.'—'Is he your son?' I asked, stepping up.—'Yes indeed, my poor son!' she responded. 'God has given me a terrible cross to bear.'—'How long has he been like this?' I asked.—'He has been as calm as this for just six months,' she said. 'Thanks be to God that he has recovered this much. Before, he was raving for a full year and they kept him in chains in the madhouse. Now he won't do anyone any harm, he just goes on about kings and emperors all the time. He was such a good and peaceable fellow, helped to maintain me, wrote a very fine hand, and suddenly he fell to brooding, was taken with a violent fever, and then grew frenzied, and now he is as you see him. If I were only to tell you, sir . . .'—I interrupted this flood of words by inquiring: 'And when was this period he tells of, when he was so happy and contented?' —'The foolish fellow!' she exclaimed, with a pitying smile. 'He means when he was out of his wits; that was the time he speaks so fondly of, when he was in the madhouse and totally unaware of a thing.'—This struck me like a thunderbolt; I pressed a coin into her hand and hastened away.

That time when you were happy! I shouted, hurrying towards the town, that time when you were thoroughly contented!—Dear God in heaven, was this the Fate Thou hast ordained for Man: that he should only be happy before he has yet attained his reason, or after he has lost it again?—Miserable wretch! and yet I envy your melancholy, and the confusion of your senses that has laid you waste! Hopefully you go forth—in winter—to pick flowers for your queen, and are sad when you cannot find any, and cannot understand why there are none. And I—I go out with no hope or purpose at all, and return home as I departed.—You have a notion of the man you might be if the general estates paid you. Happy creature, who can think some obstacle in the world about you the cause of your woes! You do not sense, no, you do not sense that your wretchedness lies within, in your ruined heart and shattered mind, and all the kings on earth cannot help you.

Let them end their days miserably who would mock a sick man who journeys to a far-off spring, perhaps only to find his sickness grown worse and the pains of his departing the greater! or who look down on some poor heart, beset with sore trials, who makes a pilgrimage to the holy sepulchre to allay the pangs of conscience and alleviate the sorrows of the soul. Every sore and painful step he takes on the untrodden path affords another drop of balm to his frighted soul, and after every day's journey he endures he goes to his rest with a lighter heart, freed of many troubles.—And dare you call it lunacy, you pack of scribblers lounging on your cushions?—Lunacy!—Oh God,

103

Thou seest my tears! Didst Thou, who created Man the poorest of creatures, didst Thou needs must give him brothers to rob him of the little he has, and take away what trust he has in Thee, who lovest everything! For what is our trust in the healing power of a root, or in the juice of the grape, but trust in Thee, who hast given us, in all that surrounds us, the healing and restorative powers we are constantly in need of? Father, whom I know not! Father, who used to fill my entire soul and who hast now turned Thy face from me, summon me to Thee! Be silent no more! Thy silence cannot delay my thirsting soul—What man, what father, could be wrathful if his son returned home[63] unexpectedly, fell at his breast and cried: 'I am here again, dear father! Do not be angry with me for breaking off my travels, which you wished me to persevere in longer. It is everywhere the same in this world, toil and labour, joys and rewards; what of it? I am only contented in your presence, and I shall suffer or enjoy here before you.'—And shouldst Thou, dear Father in heaven, turn that son from Thy sight?

1 December

Wilhelm! The man I wrote to you of, that happy unfortunate, was a clerk in Lotte's father's employ, and what drove him mad was a passion for her, which he nurtured, kept secret, then revealed to her, and which cost him his position. You will feel, as you read these unemotional words, how greatly the story affected my mind; Albert told it me, in as tranquil a spirit as you will perhaps read it.

4 December

I beg you—It is all over with me, Wilhelm, I cannot stand it any longer! Today I was sitting with her—I sat there, and she was playing the piano, various melodies, and all of it so expressive! all of it!—all!—Wilhelm!—Her little sister was dressing her doll on my knee. The tears came to my eyes. I bent forward, and my eye was caught by her wedding ring, and the tears flowed—And all of a sudden she began to play that old tune, so full of divine sweetness, quite suddenly, and my soul was filled with a sense of solace, and with memories of past times when I heard that air and of the dejected gloom and disappointed hopes since those times, and—I paced to and fro in the parlour, my heart smothering in its affliction.—'For God's sake,' I said fiercely, stepping towards her, 'stop it, for God's sake!'—She stopped playing, and stared at me. 'Werther,' she said, with a smile that pierced my soul, 'you are ill, Werther, very ill: you cannot stomach your favourite dishes. Go, I implore you, and calm down.'—I tore myself away and—dear God! Thou seest my misery and wilt make an end of it.

6 December

How her figure haunts me! Waking or dreaming, she fills my entire soul! Here in my head, in my mind's eye, I see her dark eyes the moment I close my own. Here!—I do not know how to put it. The second I close my eyes I see hers before me, deep as an ocean or an abyss, and they are within me, filling the senses of my mind.

What a thing is Man, this lauded demi-god! Does he not lack the very powers he has most need of? And if he should soar in joy, or sink in sorrow, is he not halted and returned to his cold, dull consciousness at the very moment he was longing to be lost in the vastness of infinity?

I wish very much that we had enough of our friend's own testimony, concerning the last remarkable days of his life, to render it unnecessary for me to interrupt this series of preserved letters with narration.

I have seen it as my duty to gather precise information from the mouths of those likely to be best acquainted with his history; it is a simple story, and all of the accounts agree except on a few insignificant details; though opinions and judgements vary with respect to the fundamental attitudes of the people involved.

We have no alternative but conscientiously to relate what repeated endeavours have brought to light, to include letters written by the deceased, and to attend to even the slightest scrap of paper we have found; especially as it is so difficult to discern the true and peculiar motives of even a single action of men who are not of a common order.

Discontent and sorrow had struck ever deeper roots in Werther's soul, had taken a tighter hold, and had gradually affected his entire being. The harmony of his spirit was completely destroyed, and a fever and frenzy within him, which confounded his natural powers, produced the most disagreeable effects, and at length left him in a state of exhaustion, from which he tried to fight free in a greater panic than had marked any of his previous struggles with misfortune. The anxiety in his heart sapped his remaining mental vigour, his vitality and his insight; he became a melancholy companion, his unhappiness ever increasing, the injustice of his behaviour increasing in proportion to his unhappiness. This, at least, is what Albert's friends say; they claim that Werther, who (as it were) spent every day laying waste his own powers and languishing in misery in the evenings, was unable to appreciate a quiet and pure-hearted man such as Albert, who was finally enjoying the happiness he had long looked forward to and whose conduct was intended to preserve that happiness in future too.

Albert, they say, had not undergone any change in so short a time, and was still the man Werther had known from the start, the man he had valued and respected so greatly. He loved Lotte above all else, was proud of her, and wanted everyone to acknowledge that she was the most splendid of beings. Could he be blamed for wishing to avert even the merest breath of suspicion, and for being unprepared at that time to share his exquisite prize with anyone, even in the most innocent of ways? They concede that Albert often left his wife's room when Werther was in her company, but say that he did so not out of hatred or aversion towards his friend but because he sensed that Werther found his presence oppressive.

Lotte's father was indisposed and confined to his room; he sent his carriage, and Lotte went to see him. It was a fine winter day, and the first snow had fallen, blanketing the surrounding country to some depth.

Werther went after her the following morning, in order to accompany her home if Albert did not go to collect her.

The beautiful weather had barely any effect on his low spirits, his soul was stifled and oppressed, images of melancholy had taken possession of him, and there was no change in his spirit other than from one painful thought to the next.

Living as he did in a state of constant distress, he found the condition of others increasingly cause for concern and bewilderment, supposed he had upset the delightful harmony Albert enjoyed with his wife, and reproached himself for having done so, at the same time harbouring a secret resentment of the husband.

As he walked, his thoughts turned to this question. 'Yes, yes,' he said to himself, grinding his teeth, 'there you have this tender, friendly, intimate manner, full of sympathy, this calm and constant loyalty! It is merely smugness and indifference! His wretched business affairs draw him more strongly than his dear and precious wife! Does he value his own happiness? Does he honour and respect her as she deserves? Well, she is his, yes, she is his—I know it, just as I know something else as well, and imagine I am used to the idea, but it will drive me crazy, it will be the end of me—And did his friendship stand the test? Does he not in fact see my affection for Lotte as an infringement of his rights, and my attentiveness to her as an unvoiced rebuke? All too well I know, and feel, that he does not

107

like seeing me there and wishes I were gone, my presence is a nuisance.'

Repeatedly he paused in his rapid stride, repeatedly he stood still and seemed to be thinking of turning back; but every time he proceeded on his way, and at length, occupied with these thoughts and soliloquies, he reached the hunting lodge, against his better judgement, as it were.

He entered, and inquired after the old gentleman and Lotte; the household proved to be in a state of turmoil. The eldest boy told him that over in Wahlheim a tragedy had happened, a peasant had been murdered!—The news made no great impression on him.—He entered the parlour and found Lotte busy reasoning with her father, who, in spite of his illness, wanted to go over and make investigations at the scene of the crime. As yet the identity of the murderer was unknown; the dead man had been found at his front door that morning; but there were suspicions, since the murdered man had been in the service of a widow who had previously had another servant who had left her house in strife.

On hearing this, Werther reacted with some violence.—'Can it be possible!' he exclaimed. 'I must go across, I cannot delay for a single moment.'—He hurried towards Wahlheim, every memory vividly before him, not doubting for an instant that the man who had committed the deed was the same he had sometimes spoken to and whom he had come to esteem.

To reach the inn, where the body had been carried, he had to pass the linden trees, and now he felt horror for the place he had loved so dearly. That threshold where the children of the neighbourhood had so often played was splashed with blood. Love and constancy, the most beautiful of human emotions, had been transformed into violence and murder. The mighty trees were bare of foliage and touched with frost, the beautiful hedges that crowned the low churchyard wall were leafless, and the gravestones, covered in snow, could be seen through the gaps.

As he approached the inn, where the whole village had assembled, a great commotion suddenly broke out. In the distance a troop of armed men could be made out, and everyone was shouting that the murderer had been caught. Werther looked, and was not long in doubt. Indeed, it was the servant who so fondly loved the widow, whom he had happened upon recently, wandering about in silent rage and in deep despair.

'You wretched man, what have you done!' cried Werther, advancing on the prisoner.—The captive gazed at him calmly, remained silent, and then at length, with utter composure, replied: 'No one will have her, and she will have no one.'—The prisoner was taken into the inn, and Werther hastened away.

This horrifying, violent occurrence had profoundly disturbed the whole of his being. For a moment he was torn from his melancholy, moroseness and resigned indifference; sympathy took an irresistible hold on him, and he was seized by an inexpressible longing to save the man. He felt him to be so unhappy, even as a criminal he considered him so blameless, and he was so able to see things through the man's eyes, that he felt sure he could persuade others to view the matter the same way. Already he wanted to speak in his defence, and his lips were already forming the most animated of statements as he hurried towards the hunting lodge, and as he went he could not help voicing in low tones all the things he wanted to tell the estate officer.

When he entered the parlour he found Albert present, and for a moment he was put out; but he quickly regained his composure and gave the officer a heated account of his views. The latter shook his head a number of times, and, although Werther urged everything a man can say in another's defence, and did so with the greatest possible liveliness, passion and truthfulness, the officer nevertheless remained unmoved, as may readily be imagined. Indeed, rather than permit our friend to finish what he was saying he contradicted him vigorously and reproved him for taking the part of a base murderer; he showed him that that was the way to render every law useless and destroy the security of the state; and he added that he could do nothing in such a case without assuming the gravest responsibility, and everything would have to take its usual orderly course, in the prescribed channels.

Werther did not give up yet, but requested the officer to turn a blind eye if someone were to help the fellow escape! The officer rejected this proposal too. Albert, finally joining in the conversation, took the side of the old gentleman too. Werther was out-voted, and, consumed with dreadful sorrow, took his leave, the officer first having told him a number of times: 'No, he cannot be saved!'

The impact these words must have had on him can be seen from a note that was found among his papers and which was doubtless written that very day:

You cannot be saved, unfortunate man! I well see that we cannot be saved.

What Albert had said concerning the matter of the prisoner, in the presence of the officer, struck Werther as highly unpleasant, and he thought he had detected an aversion to himself in it; and although, on repeated consideration, it did not escape his keen perception that the two men might well be in the right, he none the less felt that to concede the point and admit as much would be a renunciation of his inmost self.

Among his papers there is a note that relates to this question and perhaps summarizes his relations with Albert:

What use is it if I repeat over and over again that he is a good and worthy man? It is tearing my very heart in two; I cannot be just.

It was a mild evening, and a thaw was approaching, so Lotte and Albert returned on foot. During the walk, she looked about her at points, for all the world as if she missed Werther's company. Albert began to speak of him, and, remaining scrupulously fair, censured Werther. He touched upon his unhappy passion, and wished it were possible to be rid of him.—'I wish it for our own sakes, too,' he said, and continued: 'and I'd ask you to see that he behaves rather differently towards you, and cuts down on these frequent visits. People are starting to notice, and I know that here and there it is talked about.'—Lotte was silent, and Albert seemed to feel her silence; at all events, from that time he no longer made any mention of Werther to her, and if she did so he either dropped the conversation or changed the subject.

The vain attempt Werther had made to save the unfortunate man was the last flaring up of a dying flame; subsequently he sank all the more deeply into a state of inactivity and pain, and was particularly distraught, almost beside himself, on hearing that he might be summoned as a witness against the man, who was now denying everything.

All of the unpleasant things he had experienced in the course of an active life, his mortification during his period spent with the ambassador, everything he had failed in or which had grieved him, he now turned over in his soul. All of it seemed a vindication of inactivity; he felt cut off from all his prospects, incapable of taking a grip on the affairs of everyday life; and so, wholly abandoned to his own remarkable sensibility and way of thinking and an unremitting passion, perpetuating the same unvarying and melancholy association with the amiable and beloved creature whose peace of mind he was ruining, squandering his powers in aimless and pointless efforts, he steadily approached his tragic end.

His confusion, his passion, his restless energies and endeavours, and his weariness of life, are most powerfully attested in a few surviving letters which we interpolate at this point.

12 December

Dear Wilhelm, I am in the condition that those wretches must have been in who were said to be possessed of an evil demon. Sometimes it takes hold of me: not any fear or desire, but an unfamiliar tumult within, which chokes me and threatens to tear my heart asunder! Alas, alas!—and then I go wandering amidst the terrible night-time scenes of a season that is so hostile to Man.

Yesterday evening I had to go out. A thaw had suddenly set in, I had heard that the river had burst its banks, all the streams were swollen, and all the way from Wahlheim my beloved valley was flooded! It was after eleven, and I ran out into the night. It was a fearful spectacle: the raging torrents were crashing down from the crags in the moonlight, flooding the fields and meadows and hedges, and the broad valley, upstream and down, was a turbulent lake whipped by a roaring wind! And when the moon appeared once more, peaceful above a sombre cloud, and the flood before me rolled and thundered and gleamed with awesome majesty, a shudder of horror shook me—and then longing seized me again! Ah, there I stood, arms outstretched, above the abyss, breathing:

plunge! plunge!—and was lost in the joyful prospect of ending my sufferings and sorrows by plunging, passing on with a crash like the waves! But oh!—I could not move an inch from where I stood, I could not put an end to my torment!—My time has not yet come, I can sense it! Oh Wilhelm! how gladly I should have surrendered my human existence in order to be that stormy wind, scattering the clouds, snatching at the floods! Ha!—May that rapture not still lie ahead for this imprisoned soul?

Sadly I looked down at a spot where Lotte and I rested beneath a willow on a hot day's walk—it was under water too, and I could scarcely make out the willow tree! Wilhelm! And her meadows, I thought, and the country around her lodge! How the bower will have been ruined by these raging floods! I thought. And a ray of sunshine from the past shone down on me, just as a dream of flocks or meadows or honorary offices may shine upon a prisoner. There I stood!—I am not angry with myself, because I do have the courage to die. Or perhaps I have it.—So now here I sit like an old woman who gathers her firewood from fences and goes begging at doors for bread, to drag out her joyless, dying existence one moment longer and make it easier to bear.

14 December

What does it mean, dear friend? I alarm myself! Is not my love for her the most sacred, purest and most brotherly love? Have I ever harboured reprehensible desires in my soul?—Not that I want to claim—And these dreams!—How truly Man's sense guided him when he ascribed contradictory effects to outside agencies! I tremble to tell you, but last night! last night I held her in my arms, pressed her to my breast, and covered her lips with countless kisses while she murmured of her love; and my eyes misted to see the rapture in hers! Dear God! is it a sin to feel that happiness even now, and to recall those ardent pleasures with the greatest of joy? Lotte! Lotte!—It is all over with me! My senses are confused, for a full week I have been unable to think straight, my eyes are full of tears. Nowhere do I feel at ease, and yet I am content everywhere. I wish for nothing, and make no demands. It would be better if I were gone.

His decision to quit the world had been ever more powerfully confirmed in Werther's soul during this period and in these circumstances. Ever since his return to Lotte, that thought had constantly been his final option, his final hope; yet he had resolved that it should not be an overhasty and impetuous deed, but rather the step should be taken out of conviction and with as calm a determination as possible.

That he was filled with doubts and at odds with himself is shown by an undated note that was found among his papers and which was probably the beginning of a letter to Wilhelm:

Her presence, and her fate, and the sympathy she has for mine, are extracting the very last tears from my anguished spirit.

To lift the curtain and step behind it!—That is all! Why these doubts and hesitation? Because one does not know what lies beyond? and because one cannot return?[64] It is characteristic of our human spirit to suspect that all is confusion and darkness where we know nothing for certain.

At length he had grown familiar and acquainted with the melancholy thought, and his resolve was firm and irreversible, as is proved by the following ambiguous letter written to his friend.

20 December

I thank you for the love you show, dear Wilhelm, in picking up my words. Yes, you are right: it would be better if I were gone. I am not entirely pleased by your proposal that I return to stay with you; I should at least like to make a roundabout return of it, since we can expect the frosty weather to continue and the roads to be good. I welcome your plan to come and collect me; but perhaps you would delay for another fortnight, and wait for another letter from me, with further details. One ought not to pick the fruit before it is ripe.

And a fortnight either way can make a great difference. Be so good as to request my mother to pray for her son, and tell her I beg her forgiveness for the distress I have caused her. It seems it has been my fate to sadden those I should have made happy. Farewell, my dearest friend! May heaven send you every blessing! Farewell!

We scarcely feel able to express in words what was happening in Lotte's soul at this time, or to describe her feelings towards her husband and her unfortunate friend; although our knowledge of her character makes it possible to conceive of them, and any sensitive female soul will be in a position to enter into Lotte's frame of mind and share her emotions.

One thing is certain: that she was quite determined to do everything she could to remove Werther from her presence; and any hesitation was due to her heartfelt wish to spare her friend, since she knew how much it would cost him, and indeed that he would find it well-nigh impossible. Yet during this period she was under increased pressure to be firm; her husband maintained a complete silence concerning the relationship, just as she herself had also always been silent on the subject, and so she felt all the more need to prove by her actions that her feelings were worthy of her husband's respect.

On the same day that Werther wrote this last-quoted letter to his friend, the Sunday before Christmas, he called on Lotte in the evening, and found her alone. She was busy fixing a number of playthings she had made for her little brothers and sisters as Christmas presents. He spoke of the delight the children would feel, and of times gone by when the unexpected opening of a door to reveal a Christmas tree decorated with candles, sweets and apples sent one into transports of paradisic joy.—'If you behave well,' said Lotte, hiding her embarrassment under a gentle smile, 'if you behave yourself, you shall have a present too, a taper, and something else.'—'And what do you mean by behaving myself?' he exclaimed. 'How am I to be? How can I be? Dearest Lotte!'—'Thursday evening,' she said, 'is Christmas Eve, and the children will all be here, and my father too; there is a present for everyone; and you must come too—but not before then.'—This brought Werther up short.—'I implore you,' she continued; 'that is the way things are: I implore you for the sake of my own peace of mind; this cannot, cannot go on.'—He averted his gaze from her and paced up and down the parlour, muttering between his teeth: 'This cannot go on!'—Lotte, who sensed the terrible state her words had put him in, tried to distract his thoughts by asking all kinds of questions, but in vain. —'No, Lotte,' he cried, 'I shall never see you again!'—'Why ever not?' she replied; 'Werther, you may and must see us again, but do be less agitated in your manner. Oh, why did you have to be born with this intense spirit, this uncontrollable passion for everything you are close to! I implore you,' she went on, taking his hand, 'be calmer. Think of the many joys your spirit, your knowledge and your gifts afford you! Be a man. Put an end to this dismal attachment to a creature who can do nothing but pity you.'—He ground his teeth and gazed at her sombrely. She continued to hold his hand.—'Be calm for just a moment, Werther,' she said. 'Do you not sense that you are deceiving yourself and willing your own destruction? Why me of all people, Werther? I belong to another, so why me? I fear, I very much fear that what makes the desire to possess me so attractive is its very impossibility.'—He withdrew his hand from hers and stared at her with an affronted look. 'How wise!' he exclaimed. 'How very wise! I suppose that was one of Albert's remarks? Clever! Very clever!' —'Anyone might have said it,' she responded. 'Can there really not be another girl in the whole wide world to satisfy the longings of your heart? Take a grip on yourself, and go in search of her, and I swear you will find her; I have for some time been worried, on your account and ours, by the narrow confinement you have imposed on yourself of late. Be firm with yourself. Go on your travels: it will and must take your mind off things. Seek someone who is worthy of your love, find her, and then return, and we shall enjoy the happiness of true friendship together.'

'That speech,' he remarked, with a cold laugh, 'could be printed and commended to the use of teachers. Dear Lotte! leave me in peace just a little longer and all will be well!'—'But be sure, Werther, not to come before Christmas Eve!'—He was about to reply when Albert entered the parlour. Frostily they wished each other good evening, and then, embarrassed, walked up and down the room at each other's side. Werther started on some unimportant remarks and was soon finished, Albert did the same and then asked his wife about certain matters she had had to see to, and, on being told that she had not yet done so, made some comments to her which struck Werther as cold, indeed harsh. He wished to leave but was unable to do so, and vacillated till eight o'clock, his ill-humour and irritation mounting, till the table was laid, and he took up his hat and stick. Albert invited him to stay, but Werther, thinking it a mere formality, thanked thim coldly and left.

He returned home, took the candle from his servant, who was going to light his way, and went to his room alone, where he wept loudly, talked excitedly to himself, paced agitatedly up and down the room, and finally flung himself on the bed, still wearing his clothes; his servant found him there shortly before eleven when he ventured to enter the room, and asked if he should take off sir's boots, which Werther permitted him to do, then forbidding the servant to enter the room the next morning before he was summoned.

On the morning of Monday, 21 December, he wrote the following letter to Lotte, which was found sealed on his desk after his death and given to her; I shall quote it here one fragment at a time, since the circumstances suggest that that is how he wrote it.

The decision is taken, Lotte, I am resolved to die, and I am writing the words to you without any romantic hysteria but calmly, on the morning of the day I shall see you for the last time. When you read this, my precious, the cool grave will already hold the rigid remains of the troubled unfortunate who can conceive of no sweeter pleasure in the final moments of his life than talking to you. I have spent a terrible night, but ah! it was a good night, for it gave me a firm determination in my purpose: I am resolved to die! When I tore myself away from you yesterday, with all my senses in fearful upheaval and my heart oppressed, and confronted coldly and appallingly by the joyless hopelessness of existence near to you—I was scarcely about to reach my room, and threw myself down on my knees, beside myself—and Thou gavest me, oh God! the last consolation of shedding bitter tears! A thousand possibilities and plans raged in my soul, but in the end it was there, one last, fixed and definite thought: I am resolved to die!—I lay down, and in that peaceful morning hour of awakening the decision was still unshaken, its power undiminished in my heart: I am resolved to die!—It is not despair; I am convinced I have endured my fill of sorrows, and that I am sacrificing myself for you. Yes, Lotte! why should I not say it? One of us three must go, so let it be me! Oh, my dearest one! this broken heart of mine has often harboured furious thoughts of—killing your husband!—or you!—or myself!—So be it!—When you climb the mountainside some fine summer evening, remember me, the way I would come walking up the valley, and then look over to the churchyard, to my grave, with the wind waving the long grass in the light of the setting sun.—I was composed when I began writing, but now, now I see it all too vividly, and I am crying like a child.—

Soon before ten o'clock, Werther summoned his servant, and, while he was dressing, told him that he would be setting out on a journey in a few days' time, and asked him to brush his clothes and lay out his things for packing; he also ordered him to call in all his bills, collect books he had lent out and pay their due share for two months ahead to a number of poor people he gave alms to every week.

He had lunch brought to his room, and after eating rode out to see the estate officer, but did not find him at home. He walked about the garden deep in thought, seeming at the very end to want to absorb the whole melancholy of recollection.

The children did not leave him in peace for long, and chased after him, jumped up on him, and told him that the day after the day after tomorrow they would be getting their Christmas presents from Lotte, and told him of the wonderful things their little imaginations were looking forward to.—'Tomorrow!' he exclaimed; 'and the day after! and the day after that!'—and he kissed every one of them heartily and was on the point of leaving when the little one said he wanted to whisper something else in his ear. And he let Werther into the secret that his big brothers had written out lists of beautiful New Year wishes, ever such long lists!—one for Papa, one for Albert and Lotte, and one for Mr Werther too; they were going to present them on New Year's morning. This was too much for Werther, and, giving each of the children a present, he mounted his horse, left good wishes for the old gentleman and rode away with tears in his eyes.

He returned home shortly before five, ordered the maid to see to the fire, and told her to keep it burning late into the night. He ordered his servant to pack books and linen at the bottom of his trunk, and to sew his clothing into protective covers. It was probably at this point that he wrote the following paragraph of his final letter to Lotte.

117

You do not expect me! You suppose I will obey, and not see you again until Christmas Eve. Oh, Lotte! it must be today or never again. On Christmas Eve you will hold this page in your hand, trembling, and shed your tender tears on it. I will, I must! Oh, how good it feels to be so determined.

Lotte was meanwhile in a singular frame of mind. After her last conversation with Werther she had felt how hard she would find it to part from him, and had sensed how he would suffer if he were to part from her.

It had been mentioned in Albert's presence, more or less in passing, that Werther would not be calling again before Christmas Eve; and Albert had ridden out to see an official in the neighbour-hood with whom he had business affairs to conduct. He would have to stay the night there.

She now sat alone, with none of her brothers or sisters about her, immersed in thoughts of her own which dwelt on those who were dear to her. She was now united for all eternity with the man whose love and fidelity she knew so well, to whom she was devoted with all her heart, and whose tranquillity and reliability seemed intended by heaven for an honest woman to found her worldly happiness on; and she could feel what he would always mean to herself and the children. On the other hand, Werther had become most precious to her, from the very first moment of their acquaintance there had been so beautiful a harmony in their spirits, and their long-lasting association and various situations they had experienced had made an indelible impression on her heart. She was accustomed to sharing every thought and feeling that interested her with him, and his departure threatened to tear open a void in her being that could not be filled again. Oh, if only she might have transformed him into a brother at that moment, how happy she would have been! If only she could have had him marry one of her friends, she would have been able to hope for a complete improvement in his relations with Albert too!

She had reviewed all her women friends in her mind, and had found fault with every one of them and could hit upon none that she would want to see him with.

All of these reflections prompted a profound realization, albeit one which she was not consciously aware of, that her secret heart's desire was to keep him for herself, yet at the same time she reminded herself that she could not and might not keep him; her pure and beautiful nature, which at other times was so lighthearted and readily found a way out of predicaments, sensed the oppressive power of melancholy, banishing the prospect of happiness. Her heart was heavy, and her vision was clouded by sadness.

It was half past six by the time she heard Werther coming up the stairs; she quickly recognized his step, and his voice asking after her. Her heart beat wildly upon his arrival; indeed, it may not be too much to say it did so for the first time. She would have preferred to have him told she was out, and, when he entered, she exclaimed in impassioned distraction: 'You did not keep your word.'—'I promised nothing,' was his reply.—'Even so, you should at least have respected my request,' she pursued; 'I asked you to give us both some peace.'

She did not well know what she was saying, nor what she was doing, when she then sent for some friends, so that she would not be alone with Werther. He put down some books he had brought, asked after some others; and one moment she wished her friends would come, the next that they would stay away. The maid returned, bringing word that both of them had sent their excuses.

She thought of having the maid sit doing her work in the next room; then she thought differently of it. Werther paced up and down the parlour, and she went to the piano and began to play a minuet, but it would not come. She pulled herself together and sat down calmly at Werther's side, on the sofa where he had taken his usual place.

'Do you have nothing to read?' she said.—He did not.—'Over there in my drawer,' she went on, 'is your own translation[65] of some of the songs of Ossian; I have not read them yet, because I have always been hoping to hear you read them to me; but for some time it hasn't been possible.'—He smiled, fetched the songs, shuddered as he picked them up, and his eyes filled with tears as he opened the manuscript. He sat down and read.

Star of descending night! fair is thy light in the west! Thou liftest thy unshorn head from thy cloud; thy steps are stately on thy hill. What dost thou behold in the plain? The stormy winds are laid. The murmur of the torrent comes from afar. Roaring waves climb the distant rock. The flies of evening are on their feeble wings: the hum of their course is on the field. What dost thou behold, fair light? But thou dost smile and depart. The waves come with joy

119

around thee: they bathe thy lovely hair. Farewell, thou silent beam! Let the light of Ossian's soul arise!

And it does arise in its strength! I behold my departed friends. Their gathering is on Lora, as in the days of other years. Fingal comes like a watery column of mist! his heroes are around: and see the bards of song, grey-haired Ullin! stately Ryno! Alpin with the tuneful voice! the soft complaint of Minona! How are ye changed, my friends, since the days of Selma's feast! when we contended, like gales of spring as they fly along the hill, and bend by turns the feebly whistling grass.

Minona came forth in her beauty, with downcast look and tearful eye. Her hair was flying slowly with the blast that rushed unfrequent from the hill. The souls of the heroes were sad when she raised the tuneful voice. Oft had they seen the grave of Salgar, the dark dwelling of white-bosomed Colma. Colma left alone on the hill with all her voice of song! Salgar promised to come! but the night descended around. Hear the voice of Colma, when she sat alone on the hill!

COLMA

It is night: I am alone, forlorn on the hill of storms. The wind is heard on the mountain. The torrent is howling down the rock. No hut receives me from the rain: forlorn on the hill of winds!

Rise moon! from behind thy clouds. Stars of the night, arise! Lead me, some light, to the place where my love rests from the chase alone! His bow near him unstrung, his dogs panting around him! But here I must sit alone by the rock of the mossy stream. The stream and the wind roar aloud. I hear not the voice of my love! Why delays my Salgar; why the chief of the hill his promise? Here is the rock and here the tree! here is the roaring stream! Thou didst promise with night to be here. Ah! whither is my Salgar gone? With thee I would fly from my father, with thee from my brother of pride. Our race have long been foes: we are not foes, O Salgar!

Cease a little while, O wind! stream, be thou silent awhile! let my voice be heard around! let my wanderer hear me! Salgar! it is Colma who calls. Here is the tree and the rock. Salgar, my love, I am here! Why delayest thou thy coming? Lo! the calm moon comes forth. The flood is bright in the vale. The rocks are grey on the steep. I see him not on the brow. His dogs come not before him with tidings of his near approach. Here I must sit alone!

Who lie on the heath beside me? Are they my love and my brother? Speak to me, O my friends! To Colma they give no reply. Speak to me: I am alone! My soul is tormented with fears. Ah, they are dead! Their swords are red from the fight. O my brother! my brother! why hast thou slain my Salgar! Why, O Salgar, hast thou slain my brother! Dear were ye both to me! What shall I say in your praise? Thou wert fair on the hill among thousands! he was terrible in fight! Speak to me! hear my voice! hear me, sons of my love! They are silent! silent for ever! Cold, cold, are their breasts of clay! Oh, from the rock on the hill, from the top of the windy steep, speak, ye ghosts of the dead! Speak, I will not be afraid! Whither are ye gone to rest? In what cave of the hill shall I find the departed? No feeble voice is on the gale: no answer half drowned in the storm!

I sit in my grief: I wait for morning in my tears! Rear the tomb, ye friends of the dead. Close it not till Colma come. My life flies away like a dream. Why should I stay behind? Here shall I rest with my friends, by the stream of the sounding rock. When night comes on the hill—when the loud winds arise, my ghost shall stand in the blast, and mourn the death of my friends. The hunter shall hear from his booth; he shall fear, but love, my voice! For sweet shall my voice be for my friends: pleasant were her friends to Colma.

Such was thy song, Minona, softly blushing daughter of Torman. Our tears descended for Colma, and our souls were sad! Ullin came with his harp; he gave the song of Alpin. The voice of Alpin was pleasant, the soul of Ryno was a beam of fire! But they had rested in the narrow house: their voice had ceased in Selma! Ullin had returned one day from the chase before the heroes fell. He heard their strife on the hill: their song was soft, but sad! They mourned the fall of Morar, first of mortal men! His soul was like the soul of Fingal: his sword like the sword of Oscar. But he fell, and his father mourned: his sister's eyes were full of tears. Minona's eyes were full of tears, the sister of car-borne Morar. She retired from the song of Ullin, like the moon in the west, when she foresees the shower, and hides her fair head in a cloud. I touched the harp with Ullin: the song of mourning rose!

RYNO

The wind and the rain are past, calm is the noon of day. The clouds are divided in heaven. Over the green hills flies the inconstant sun. Red through the stony vale comes down the stream of the hill. Sweet are thy murmurs, O stream! but more sweet is the voice I hear. It is the voice of Alpin, the son of song, mourning for the dead! Bent is his head of age: red his tearful eye. Alpin, thou son of song, why alone on the silent hill? Why complainest thou, as a blast in the wood—as a wave on the lonely shore?

ALPIN

My tears, O Ryno! are for the dead—my voice for those that have passed away. Tall thou art on the hill; fair among the sons of the vale. But thou shalt fall like Morar: the mourner shall sit on thy tomb. The hills shall know thee no more: thy bow shall lie in thy hall unstrung!

Thou wert swift, O Morar! as a roe on the desert: terrible as a meteor of fire. Thy wrath was as the storm. Thy sword in battle as lightning in the field. Thy voice was a stream after rain, like thunder on distant hills. Many fell by thy arm: they were consumed in the flames of thy wrath. But when thou didst return from war, how peaceful was thy brow. Thy face was like the sun after rain: like the moon in the silence of night: calm as the breast of the lake when the loud wind is laid.

Narrow is thy dwelling now! dark the place of thine abode! With three steps I compass thy grave, O thou who wast so great before! Four stones, with their heads of moss, are the only memorial of thee. A tree with scarce a leaf, long grass which whistles in the wind, mark to the hunter's eye the grave of the mighty Morar. Morar! thou art low indeed. Thou hast no mother to mourn thee, no maid with her tears of love. Dead is she that brought thee forth. Fallen is the daughter of Morglan.

Who on his staff is this? Who is this whose head is white with age, whose eyes are red with tears, who quakes at every step? It is thy father, O Morar! the father of no son but thee. He heard of thy fame in war, he heard of foes dispersed. He heard of Morar's renown, why did he not hear of his wound? Weep, thou father of Morar! Weep, but thy son heareth thee not. Deep is the sleep of the dead,—low their pillow of dust. No more shall he hear thy voice,—no more awake at thy call. When shall it be morn in the grave, to bid the slumberer awake? Farewell, thou bravest of men! thou conqueror in the field! But the field shall see thee no more, nor the dark wood be lightened with the splendour of thy steel. Thou hast left no son. The song shall preserve thy name. Future times shall hear of thee—they shall hear of the fallen Morar!

The grief of all arose, but most the bursting sigh of Armin. He remembers the death of his son, who fell in the days of his youth. Carmor was near the hero, the chief of the echoing Galmal. Why burst the sigh of Armin? he said. Is there a cause to mourn? The song comes with its music to melt and please the soul. It is like soft mist that, rising from a lake, pours on the silent vale; the green flowers are filled with dew, but the sun returns in his strength, and the mist is gone. Why art thou sad, O Armin, chief of sea-surrounded Gorma?

Sad I am! nor small is my cause of woe! Carmor, thou hast lost no son; thou hast lost no daughter of beauty. Colgar the valiant lives, and Annira, fairest maid. The boughs of thy house ascend, O Carmor! but Armin is the last of his race. Dark is thy bed, O Daura! deep thy sleep in the tomb! When shalt thou wake with thy songs?—with all thy voice of music?

Arise, winds of autumn, arise: blow along the heath. Streams of the mountains, roar; roar, tempests in the groves of my oaks! Walk through broken clouds, O moon! show thy pale face at intervals; bring to my mind the night when all my children fell, when Arindal the mighty fell—when Daura the lovely failed. Daura, my daughter, thou wert fair, fair as the moon on Fura, white as the driven snow, sweet as the breathing gale. Arindal, thy bow was strong, thy spear was swift on the field, thy look was like mist on the wave, thy shield a red cloud in a storm! Armar, renowned in war, came and sought Daura's love. He was not long refused: fair was the hope of their friends.

Erath, son of Odgal, repined: his brother had been slain by Armar. He came disguised like a son of the sea: fair was his cliff on the wave, white his locks of age, calm his serious brow. Fairest of women, he said, lovely daughter of Armin! a rock not distant in the sea bears a tree on its side; red shines the fruit afar. There Armar waits for Daura. I come to carry his love! She went—she called on Armar. Naught answered, but the son of the rock. Armar, my love, my love! why tormentest thou me with fear? Hear, son of Arnart, hear! it is Daura who calleth thee. Erath, the traitor, fled laughing to the land. She lifted up her voice—she called for her brother and her father. Arindal! Armin! none to relieve you, Daura.

Her voice came over the sea. Arindal, my son, descended from the hill, rough in the spoils of the chase.

His arrows rattled by his side: his bow was in his hand, five dark-grey dogs attended his steps. He saw fierce Erath on the shore; he seized and bound him to an oak. Thick wind the thongs of the hide around his limbs; he loads the winds with his groans. Arindal ascends the deep in his boat to bring Daura to land. Armar came in his wrath, and let fly the grey-feathered shaft. It sung, it sunk in thy heart, O Arindal, my son! for Erath the traitor thou diest. The oar is stopped at once: he panted on the rock, and expired. What is thy grief, O Daura, when round thy feet is poured thy brother's blood. The boat is broken in twain. Armar plunges into the sea to rescue his Daura, or die. Suddenly a blast from a hill came over the waves; he sank, and he rose no more.

Alone, on the sea-beat rock, my daughter was heard to complain; frequent and loud were her cries. What could her father do? All night I stood on the shore: I saw her by the faint beam of the moon. All night I heard her cries. Loud was the wind; the rain beat hard on the hill. Before morning appeared, her voice was weak; it died away like the evening breeze among the grass of the rocks. Spent with grief, she expired, and left thee, Armin, alone. Gone is my strength in war, fallen my pride among women. When the storms aloft arise, when the north lifts the wave on high, I sit by the sounding shore, and look on the fatal rock.

Often by the setting moon I see the ghosts of my children; half viewless they walk in mournful conference together.

A flood of tears poured from Lotte's eyes, easing her beset heart, and interrupting Werther's song. He threw the manuscript aside, took hold of her hand and shed the bitterest of tears. Lotte leaned on her other hand, her handkerchief to her eyes. Both of them were fearfully agitated. They could sense their own wretchedness in the fates of the noble heroes; they sensed it together, and shed tears in harmony. Werther rested his feverish lips and eyes on Lotte's arm; she trembled; she wanted to go, yet pain and sympathy lay numbingly upon her like lead. She took deep breaths to revive herself, and, sobbing, asked him to go on, imploring him in very heaven's voice! Werther was shaking, his heart was fit to burst, but he took up the manuscript and read, in a voice half-broken:

Why dost thou waken me, O spring? Thy voice woos me, exclaiming, I refresh thee with heavenly dews; but the time of my decay is approaching, the storm is nigh that shall wither my leaves. Tomorrow the traveller shall come,—he shall come, who beheld me in beauty: his eye shall seek me in the field around, but he shall not find me.

The whole force of these words overwhelmed the unhappy Werther. He flung himself down before Lotte[66] in deep despair and seized her hands, pressing them to his eyes and forehead, and a premonition of his terrible intention flickered in her soul. Her senses were bewildered; she squeezed his hands and pressed them to her breast, bent towards him with feelings of deeply moved melancholy, and their warm cheeks touched. They were oblivious to the world about them. He clasped her in his arms, held her to his breast and covered her trembling, murmuring lips with fiery kisses.— 'Werther!' she cried in a choked voice, turning away from him;

125

'Werther!'—and with a feeble hand she pushed his breast from hers; 'Werther!' she exclaimed, in the self-controlled tone of the noblest sentiment.—He offered no resistance, released her from his embrace, and prostrated himself before her, distraught.—Hastily she stood up, and in a voice of anxious confusion, trembling between love and anger, told him: 'This is the last time! Werther! You will never see me again!' And, gazing upon the wretched man with the tenderest look of love, she hurried into the next room, and locked the door behind her.—Werther stretched his arms out after her, but did not dare detain her. He lay on the floor with his head resting on the sofa, and in that position he remained for over half an hour, until a noise brought him to his senses. It was the maid, who wanted to lay the table. He walked up and down the room, and, once he was alone again, went to the door of the adjoining room and called in low tones: 'Lotte! Lotte! Just one more word! Just a word of farewell!'—She made no reply.—He waited, repeated his request, and waited; then he tore himself away, and cried: 'Farewell, Lotte! For ever adieu!'

He reached the town gate. The watchmen were used to his habits and let him pass in silence. A fine sleet was falling, and it was not until shortly before eleven that he knocked at the door. His servant noticed that when Werther returned home he did not have his hat. He did not venture to make any comment and helped him out of his clothes, which were wet through. The hat was later found on a rock, where a hillside crag overlooks the valley, and it is inconceivable how he should have climbed it on a dark, wet night without falling.

He went to bed and slept late. His servant found him writing when, on being summoned, he took him his breakfast the next morning. Werther was writing the following addition to the letter to Lotte:

For the last time, then, for the last time I open these eyes. Ah, never more will they behold the sun; they are clouded by cheerless mists. Then mourn, Nature! for your son and friend and lover is nearing his end. Lotte, it is an incomparable feeling, and yet it is like a half-waking dream, to say to oneself: this is my last morning. The last! Lotte, I have no sense of what the word means: the last! Am I not here now with all my powers, and tomorrow I shall be sprawled on the ground, bereft of the energies of life. To die!—what does it mean? When we speak of death we are only dreaming. I have seen

126

people die; but there are such constraints on human nature that we have no feeling for the beginning and ending of our existence. Now I am still my own—yours! yours, oh my beloved! One single moment—of severance, of parting—perhaps for ever?—No, Lotte, no—how can I be annihilated? how can you be annihilated? We exist!—Annihilation!—What does it mean? It is merely another word, an empty sound, and cannot touch my heart.—Dead, Lotte! and interred in the cold earth, in the dark and narrow grave!—I had a friend who meant everything to me when I was a youth and knew nothing of life; she died, and I followed behind the body, and stood by the grave as they lowered the coffin, and heard the ropes whirr as they were quickly pulled through and up; and then the first clod was shovelled in, and the fearful coffin returned a hollow sound which grew ever more muffled, until at last it was covered! —I flung myself on the ground beside the grave—moved and torn apart within, smitten with fear, shattered, and yet I did not grasp what was happening, nor what lay ahead of me—To die! The grave! I do not understand the words!

Oh, forgive me! forgive me! Yesterday! It ought to have been the very last moment in my life. Oh, you angel! For the first time, for the very first time, without any doubt at all, I was burning deep within, burning with joy, knowing: she loves me! She loves me! The sacred fire they received from yours is still aflame on my lips, and a new and ardent joy is in my heart. Forgive me! forgive me!

Ah, I knew that you loved me, knew it from your first soulful looks, the first pressure of your hand, but once I was absent once more, and saw Albert at your side, I was disheartened again and fell a prey to feverish doubts.

Do you remember the flowers you sent me, that time you were unable to say a word to me or give me your hand in that crowded gathering? Oh, I knelt before them half the night, and to my mind they sealed your love. But ah! they were passing impressions, just as the sense of God's mercy gradually passes from the soul of a believer—that mercy which a bountiful heaven granted him through sacred and visible signs.

All of it passes away; but a whole eternity will not extinguish that living fire I enjoyed on your lips yesterday, and which I feel burning within me! She loves me! These arms held her, these lips trembled

127

against hers, this mouth murmured upon hers. She is mine! You are mine! yes, Lotte, for all eternity.

Albert is your husband—well, what of it? Husband! In the eyes of the world—and in the eyes of the world is it sinful for me to love you, to want to tear you from his embrace into my own? Sin? Very well, and I am punishing myself; I have tasted the whole divine delight of that sin, and have taken balm and strength into my heart. From this moment you are mine! mine, oh Lotte! I am going on ahead! going unto my Father,[67] your Father. I shall tell Him my sorrows and He will comfort me until that time when you come and I fly to meet you, hold you and remain with you in a perpetual embrace in the sight of the Eternal.

I am not dreaming or raving! As I approach the grave I see things more clearly. There will be a life for us! and we shall see each other again! We shall see your mother! I shall see her, I shall find her, and ah, I shall pour out all my heart to her! Your mother, the image of you.

About eleven o'clock Werther asked his servant if Albert had returned. The servant replied that he had, since he had seen his horse led past. At this, his master gave him an unsealed note to deliver, which read as follows:

Would you be so kind as to lend me your pistols for a journey I am about to make? Farewell![68]

Lotte had slept little that last night; all of her fears had been confirmed, in a way that she could have neither foreseen nor avoided. Her pure and untroubled blood was feverishly agitated, and a thousand different feelings rent her virtuous heart. Was it the fire of Werther's embraces that she felt in her bosom? Was it resentment of his outrageous behaviour? Was it the sad comparison of her present state with earlier times of ease, freedom, innocence and unruffled confidence in herself? How was she to approach her husband and confess a scene which she had no reason to conceal and which she was nevertheless loath to tell him of? They had kept their silence with each other for so long; should she be the first to break it in this untimely way by revealing so unexpected an incident to her husband? She was even afraid that the mere news of Werther's visit would make

128

an unpleasant impression on him, not to mention this unanticipated disaster! Could she hope to be seen in the correct light by her husband, and to be heard without prejudice? Could she wish, on the other hand, to have him read her inmost soul? Or again, could she offer some pretence to the man before whom she had always been as open and clear as crystal, and from whom she had never kept her feelings a secret, or been able to? The alternatives worried and embarrassed her; and repeatedly her thoughts turned to Werther, who was now lost to her, whom she could not let go of, whom she must now (alas!) leave to his own devices and who had nothing left if he had lost her.

The lack of communication which had recently prevailed between them lay heavily upon her now, though she was not fully aware of it at that moment. People as understanding and good as they turned to mutual silence on account of some inner differences, each thought himself in the right and the other in the wrong and brooded on it, and things became so complicated and volatile that it proved impossible to untie the knot at that critical moment on which everything depended. If they had been brought closer again at some earlier stage, in a spirit of happy intimacy, a mutual love and consideration would have arisen between them, and would have opened their hearts; and perhaps our friend might yet have been saved.

There was a further remarkable circumstance. Werther, as we have seen from his letters, had never made a secret of his longing to quit this world. Albert had frequently debated the question with him, and he and Lotte had also talked of it at times. Albert had a decisive aversion to the act of suicide and had often stated, with a vehemence that was uncharacteristic, that he found real cause to doubt the seriousness of Werther's intention, and he had even joked about it and told Lotte of his scepticism. It is true that this set her mind at rest, on the one hand, whenever her thoughts turned to the tragic subject; but, on the other, she felt that it prevented her from confiding in her husband the worries that tormented her at such moments.

Albert returned, and Lotte went to meet him with nervous haste; he was out of humour, his business had been left unfinished, the official he had called on in the neighbourhood had proved to be an inflexible, pusillanimous person. And the bad conditions on the road had put him further out of sorts.

He asked whether anything had happened, and she replied over-hastily that Werther had called the previous evening. He asked if any letters had come, and was told that there were a letter and some packages in his study. He then went in, and Lotte was left alone. The presence of the man she loved and honoured had kindled new feelings in her heart. The recollection of his noble spirit, goodness and love had soothed her mind, and she felt a deep impulse to follow him, took up her work, and went to his room, as she often did. She found him occupied, breaking the seals on the packages and reading. Some of them seemed hardly to contain the most agreeable news. She put a few questions, which he answered briefly, and then he stood at his writing-stand, to pen replies.

They spent an hour together in this way, and the darkness in Lotte's spirit grew deeper. She sensed how difficult she would find it to tell her husband what lay so heavily on her heart even if he were in the best of tempers; she lapsed into a melancholy gloom that upset her the more deeply, the more she tried to hide it and swallow her tears.

The appearance of Werther's servant caused her the greatest embarrassment; he handed Albert the note, and the latter turned coolly to his wife and said: 'Give him the pistols.' To the servant he added: 'I wish him a pleasant journey.'—This struck her like a thunderbolt; she swayed as she rose, and did not know what she was about. Slowly she went to the wall and took down the pistols with a shaking hand, dusted them off, and hesitated, and would have hesitated longer if Albert had not hastened her with a questioning glance. She handed the fateful implements to the servant, unable to utter a word, and once he had left the house she packed up her work and retired to her room in an inexpressible quandary. Her heart was filled with terrible forebodings. One moment she was on the point of casting herself at her husband's feet and confessing the entire history of the previous evening, where she had been at fault and what she feared. The next she perceived that nothing would result from the venture, and least of all could she hope to persuade her husband to go to see Werther. The table was laid; a good friend who had only stopped by to ask something and was going right away—and then stayed—made conversation at table bearable; they took just a little more, they talked, they told stories and everything else was forgotten.

The servant delivered the pistols, and Werther took them from him enraptured on hearing that it was Lotte who gave them to him. He ordered bread and wine, sent his servant to lunch and sat down to write.

They have been through your hands, you wiped the dust off them, I kiss them a thousand times, you touched them! Thou, Spirit of heaven, lookest upon my resolve with favour, and you, Lotte, hand me the implements, you at whose hands I desired my death, and from whom, ah! I now receive it. Oh, I asked my servant every detail. You shook as you handed them to him, and bade me no farewell!—Alas! alas! you bade me no farewell!—Have you closed your heart to me because of that moment that bound me to you for ever? Lotte, an entire millennium could not wipe out that sensation! and I feel you cannot hate the man who bears such passion for you.

After lunch he told his servant to pack everything, tore up a great many papers, and went out to settle a few small debts. He returned home, and then, despite the rain, went out once more beyond the gate to the count's garden, then wandered further afield, and returned at nightfall, and continued writing.

Wilhelm, I have set eyes on the fields and woods and heavens for the last time. I bid you farewell as well! My dear mother, forgive me! Comfort her, Wilhelm. God bless you. My affairs have all been put in order. Farewell! We shall see each other again, in a happier place.

I have requited you ill, Albert, but you must forgive me. I have disturbed the peace of your home and planted distrust between you. Farewell! I am going to make an end of it. Oh, if only my death might make you both happy! Albert! Albert! make that angel happy! May God's blessing be upon you.

That evening he sorted out his papers, tore up a great deal and threw it into the stove, and sealed a number of bundles which he addressed to Wilhelm. These contained short essays and stray reflections, various of which I have seen. He had the fire made up at ten, and had a bottle of wine brought to him, then dismissed his servant, whose room was at the far back of the house, as was the family bedroom; the servant lay down on his bed without undressing, in order to be up and doing at an early hour, since his master had said the post-horses would be at the door before six o'clock.

Past eleven

All around me is so silent, and my soul is so calm. I thank Thee, God, for granting this warmth and strength in my last moments.

I step to the window, dearest, and through the tempestuous clouds being driven by I can see, I can still see a few of the stars of eternal heaven. No, the stars will not fall! The Eternal One bears them in His heart, as he bears me. I can see the stars that make the shaft of the Plough, my favourite of all the heavenly bodies. When I used to leave you at night, and step out through your gate, it would be there above me. Often I have gazed at it, drunk with rapture, and often I have raised my hands to revere it as a symbol and sacred image of my present happiness! and then—But oh, Lotte, what is there that does not remind me of you! You are all about me! and, like a child, I have insatiably seized upon every little thing that you might have touched, dear saint!

And this dear silhouette profile! I am leaving it to you, Lotte, and beg you to cherish it. I have implanted a thousand thousand kisses on it, and a thousand times I have passed the time of day with it on leaving or returning home.

I have written a note to your father, requesting him to take my body into his protection. In the churchyard there are two linden trees in the far corner near the field; that is where I should like to lie.[69] He can and will do this for his friend. Do you ask it of him too. I do not mean to impose on pious Christians who might not care to lie immediately beside some poor unfortunate. Ah, I wish you would bury me by the wayside, or in a lonely valley, where the priest and Levite might call blessings upon themselves and pass by the stone that marks my grave, and the Samaritan[70] might shed a tear.

132

You see, Lotte, I do not flinch from taking the cold and terrible cup[71] from which I must drink the sleep of death! You handed it to me, and I do not hesitate. So now all! all of my life's wishes and hopes have been fulfilled. Cold and numb I knock at the brazen portals of Death.

To think that I might have enjoyed the happiness of dying for you! of sacrificing myself for you, Lotte! I should die courageously and gladly if I knew I could restore to you the joy and tranquillity of your life. But ah! it has been given to only a few noble beings to shed their blood for those they love, and by their death to create a new life a hundred times better for their friends.

I wish to be buried in these clothes, Lotte; you touched them and they are sacred; I have made the request of your father also. My soul will be keeping watch over my coffin. I do not want anyone going through my pockets. This pink ribbon you wore at your breast the first time I saw you amongst your children—oh, give them a thousand kisses, and tell them the fate of your wretched friend. The dear creatures! I can almost feel them romping about me. Ah, how attached I have been to you! How impossible it has been to leave you since that first moment!—This ribbon is to be buried with me. You gave it to me on my birthday! I could not get enough of it all!—Ah, I little thought that my path was leading me this way!—Be of peaceful heart, I implore you! Be of peaceful heart!—

They are loaded—It is striking twelve! So be it!—Lotte! Lotte, farewell! Farewell!

A neighbour saw the flash of the powder and heard the shot; but, since everything remained quiet, he thought no more about it.

Next morning at six o'clock the servant came in with a candle. He found his master on the floor, saw the pistol and the blood, called out and shook him; but Werther made no reply, and merely groaned. The servant ran to fetch a doctor and Albert. Lotte heard the doorbell being pulled and a shudder went through her. She woke her husband, they rose, the servant came in weeping and stammered out the news, and Lotte fainted away at Albert's feet.

When the surgeon reached the unfortunate man he found him on the floor, beyond hope; his pulse was still beating but his limbs were

133

powerless. He had shot himself above the right eye, blowing out his brains. To crown it all, a vein was opened in his arm; the blood flowed; he still continued to breathe.

From the blood on the back-rest of the chair it could be deduced that he committed the deed sitting at his desk, then sank to the floor, thrashing convulsively about the chair. He was found lying on his back near the window, all strength gone, fully clothed, wearing his boots and his blue coat and buff waistcoat.

The household, the neighbourhood and the entire town were in commotion. Albert entered. Werther had been laid on his bed, his head bandaged, his face already deathlike; he could not move his limbs. His lungs still produced a fearful death-rattle, one moment feebly, the next louder; his end was expected soon.

He had drunk only a single glass of the wine. *Emilia Galotti*[72] lay open on his desk.

Of Albert's consternation and Lotte's misery I shall say nothing.

The old officer arrived hastily on hearing the tidings, and kissed the dying man, shedding ardent tears. His eldest sons soon followed him on foot, threw themselves down by the bedside in immeasurable pain, kissed his hands and mouth; and the eldest, of whom he had always been fondest, kissed his lips until he expired, and then the boy had to be forcibly taken away. It was twelve midday when he died. The presence of the officer, and the precautions he took, prevented any disturbance. About eleven that night he had him buried at the place he had chosen for himself. The old gentleman and his sons followed the corpse, but Albert was unable to. There were fears for Lotte's life. Guildsmen bore the body. No priest attended him.

NOTES

In the notes that follow I am greatly indebted to Erich Trunz's commentary on the novel in the *Hamburger Ausgabe* (now published in Munich by C. H. Beck) and to Kurt Rothmann's volume of commentary and related documents (published in Stuttgart by Reclam).

1. *p. 25*. Leonore and her sister were probably inspired by Lucinde and Emilie, the daughters of Goethe's dancing instructor in Strassburg. The episode is described in Book 9 of *Dichtung und Wahrheit*.

2. *p. 25*. Goethe's great-aunt, Hofrätin Lange, lived in Wetzlar.

3. *p. 26*. Court-Attorney Meckel had laid out a garden on a slope leading down to the River Lahn, beyond the Wildbach Gate at Wetzlar. The garden was designed as a landscaped park in the English manner, then coming into favour in Germany, rather than in that geometrically precise French style which Werther finds objectionably scientific.

4. *p. 27*. The original of this spring was outside the Wildbach Gate at Wetzlar.

5. *p. 27*. In the fourteenth-century French tale, Melusine was a water-nymph or mermaid, half woman and half fish.

6. *p. 27*. Compare Genesis 24:13ff.

7. *p. 28*. Kestner observed that Goethe spent more time reading 'Homer, Pindar, etc.' during his period in Wetzlar than he did on his legal affairs.

8. *p. 29.* The girl would wear padding on her head to make the carrying less uncomfortable.

9. *p. 29.* The older woman to whom Werther's thoughts return in the course of his final letter to Lotte (see p. 127) was inspired by Canoness Susanne von Klettenberg, who was a friend, guide and confessor to Goethe in the years from 1768 to 1770 and whom he describes in Book 8 of *Dichtung und Wahrheit.*

10. *p. 30.* Charles Batteux (1713–80) was the author of the *Cours de belles lettres ou Principes de la littérature* (1747–50), which appeared in a German translation between 1756 and 1758 and at the beginning of the 1770s still enjoyed a high reputation. Robert Wood (1716–71) wrote *An Essay on the original genius and writings of Homer*, published in London in 1768 and in German translation in Frankfurt in 1773. The art theorist Roger de Piles (1635–1709) was still being reprinted in French and German editions in the 1760s. Johann Joachim Winckelmann (1717–68) had ranked as Germany's pre-eminent aesthetician since the publication in 1755 of his *Gedanken über die Nachahmung der griechischen Werke*, an eminence that was confirmed by his *Geschichte der Kunst des Alterums* (1764). Johann Georg Sulzer (1720–79) published the first part of his general theory of the fine arts in 1771. Professor Christian Gottlob Heyne (1729–1812) of the University of Göttingen was noted for his lectures on classical philology, and the manuscript the youth speaks of would probably have been a transcript of one of these lectures.

11. *p. 30.* The estate officer in the novel is modelled on Heinrich Adam Buff (1711–95), who had been the resident officer for the Teutonic Order (*Deutschorden*) in Wetzlar since 1755.

12. *p. 32.* Wahlheim is modelled on Garbenheim, near Wetzlar. When Werther gives distances, he does so in terms of walking time.

13. *p. 37.* A ball was held on 9 June 1772 at a hunting lodge in nearby Volpertshausen. Goethe drove out from Wetzlar in a

carriage with the daughters of his great-aunt, followed some time later by Kestner.

14. *p. 37.* Charlotte S. (or, as she is known for short, Lotte) is modelled on Heinrich Buff's daughter, Charlotte Sophie Henriette (1753–1828), who subsequently married Kestner. See Note 47 and the Introduction.

15. *p. 37.* This scene, Werther's first meeting with Lotte, was a great favourite with the novel's illustrators, and made a deep impression not only on Werther but also on the reading public. The extent to which Lotte was identified with her bread-cutting role is evidenced by Thackeray's burlesque:

> Werther had a love for Charlotte,
>   Such as words could never utter,
> Would you know how first he met her?
>   She was cutting bread and butter.
>
> Charlotte was a married lady,
>   And a moral man was Werther,
> And for all the wealth of Indies
>   Would do nothing that might hurt her.
>
> So he sighed and pined and ogled,
>   And his passion boiled and bubbled;
> Till he blew his silly brains out,
>   And no more was by them troubled.
>
> Charlotte, having seen his body
>   Borne before her on a shutter,
> Like a well conducted person
>   Went on cutting bread and butter.
>
> (1853)

16. *p. 39.* By Miss Jenny, Lotte probably means the heroine of Marie-Jeanne Riccoboni's *Histoire de Miss Jenny Glanville*, which appeared in German translation in 1764.

17. *p. 39.* Oliver Goldsmith's *The Vicar of Wakefield* (1766) was no

less popular in Germany than in England. Herder recommended it to Goethe in Strassburg, and it remained a favourite with Goethe throughout his life.

18. *p. 39*. The 'names of a number of our fatherland's authors' which the editor has deleted from Werther's letter are matter for conjecture, but it seems likely that the German novelists Lotte would have referred to, in the wake of Richardson, Fielding, Sterne and Goldsmith, would be Christoph Martin Wieland (1733–1813), Johann Timotheus Hermes (1738–1821) and Sophie von La Roche (1731–1807).

19. *p. 41*. Albert is modelled on Christian Kestner (1741–1800), who had been a secretary at court in Wetzlar since 1767 and later (in 1784) became a councillor and deputy archivist at the royal court in Hanover. See the Introduction.

20. *p. 43*. Since the publication of the first three cantos of his *Messias* in 1748, Friedrich Gottlieb Klopstock (1724–1803) had ranked as one of Germany's pre-eminent poets. His rhapsodic tone and treatment of Nature and love appealed particularly strongly to young people of Werther's and Lotte's generation. The ode which the spring rain reminds Lotte of is 'Die Frühlingsfeier' ('Celebration of Spring'), written in 1759.

21. *p. 45*. *Odyssey* II, 300ff. and XX, 248ff.

22. *p. 45*. See Matthew 18:3.

23. *p. 48*. This collection of sermons, *Predigten über das Buch Jonas*, was published in 1773 by a friend of Goethe's, Johann Kaspar Lavater (1741–1801). He is referred to once again in Werther's letter of 15 September 1772. See also Note 45.

24. *p. 50*. One of Charlotte Buff's friends was Marie Anna Brandt, eldest daughter of a Wetzlar councillor and court attorney. Amalie was the name of Charlotte's youngest sister; Malchen is the affectionate diminutive of the name.

25. *p. 51*. Goethe used the same expression in a letter he wrote to Charlotte Buff on 16 June 1774.

26. *p. 51*. See Notes 53 and 65.

27. *p. 52*. See 1 Kings 17:16.

28. *p. 55*. The cutting of black silhouette profiles on a white background (or vice versa) was very popular in Goethe's day, and could even be seen as an aid to the study of physiognomy by Lavater (see Note 45). Goethe had in his keeping a silhouette of Charlotte Buff (see Note 47).

29. *p. 59*. Magdalene Ernestine Buff (1731–71) died when her second eldest daughter, Charlotte, was eighteen. A letter Kestner wrote to von Hennings on 18 November 1772 describes the devotion and authority with which Charlotte Buff took over her mother's role.

30. *p. 61*. See John 8:7.

31. *p. 61*. See Luke 10:31 and 18:11.

32. *p. 62*. See John 11:4.

33. *p. 62*. Goethe probably based this account on the case of twenty-three-year-old Anna Elisabeth Stöber, who drowned herself in Frankfurt on 29 December 1769 after being deserted by her lover.

34. *p. 64*. Werther means the fluids that were supposed to regulate the physical and mental humours.

35. *p. 64*. The episode is from 'La chatte blanche' in the *Contes de Fées* by Marie Cathérine Jumelle de Berneville, Countess of Aulnoy (?1650–1705).

36. *p. 67*. The story is in Horace (*Epistles* I, 10) and Lafontaine (*Fables* 4, 3).

37. *p. 67*. By an astonishing coincidence, 28 August was not only Goethe's own birthday but also Kestner's.

38. *p. 68*. When Goethe had returned to Frankfurt, Charlotte Buff made him a gift of a bow she had worn on her dress at the ball in Volpertshausen (see Note 13).

39. *p. 68*. A German edition of Homer's works, with parallel Latin translation, was published in Amsterdam in 1707 by J. H. Wetstein (1649–1726). Being duodecimo and therefore pocket-sized, it would be easier to carry about than the edition made by J. A. Ernesti (published in octavo format in Leipzig, 1759–64).

40. *p. 69*. Goethe left Wetzler quite suddenly and unexpectedly on 11 September 1772, following a conversation on life after death similar to that described in Werther's letter. His farewell letter to Charlotte Buff was dated 10 September.

41. *p. 73*. The ambassador is modelled on the ambassador of Braunschweig (Brunswick), von Hoefler, who was Jerusalem's superior. Book Two of the novel is based on the tragic end of Karl Wilhelm Jerusalem (1747–72), who took his own life on seeing the misery and impossibility of his love of Elisabeth Herd, a married woman. See the Introduction.

42. *p. 74*. Count C. is based on Count von Bassenheim, who was well disposed towards Jerusalem.

43. *p. 74*. Werther's inversions were not merely characteristic of his own expressive nature but, like the majestically periodic constructions he is sometimes ecstatically capable of (as in the letter of 10 May 1771), were an essential plank in the stylistic platform of the *Sturm und Drang*, and favoured not only by Werther (and Goethe) but also by Herder, Hamann and others.

44. *p. 76*. Miss von B. is modelled on Luise von Ziegler (1750–1814) and probably not, as was supposed at one time, on Maximiliane Brentano (née La Roche).

45. *p. 76.* Like his creator Goethe, Werther is not using the word 'physiognomy' loosely but with an awareness of the morphological science the word represented. Goethe was familiar with the work of C. G. Carus and E. Kretschmer and assisted his friend Lavater in the preparatory studies for his work on physiognomy, *Physiognomische Fragmente zur Beförderung der Menschenkenntnis und Menschenliebe* (1774–8). Werther's comment on kinds of noses, in his letter of 8 August 1771, is a product of physiognomic study as much as a glance at his artistic concerns.

46. *p. 76.* The notion of a falling-off from a glorious Golden Age to a later and comparatively wretched Iron Age, by various stages, was familiar to all who read the classics. In Hesiod's *Works and Days*, for example, five stages are distinguished, from the (first) Golden Age through the (third) Brazen Age to the (fifth and final) Iron Age.

47. *p. 80.* This letter is largely autobiographical. When Goethe learnt of Charlotte Buff's marriage to Christian Kestner, he wrote: 'God bless you both; you have taken me by surprise. I intended to dig a sacred grave on Good Friday and bury Lotte's silhouette in it.'

48. *p. 81.* Franz I (1708–65), Duke of Lorraine, subsequently Grand Duke of Tuscany, married Maria Theresa in 1736 and in 1745 was made German Emperor. If the baron's attire dated from that coronation, it would thus be twenty-seven years old and hopelessly out of fashion.

49. *p. 82. Odyssey* XIV.

50. *p. 92.* The combination of buff waistcoat and breeches and blue frock-coat was very fashionable in 1771 and 1772, and was worn by Jerusalem. Following the success of Goethe's novel, it was for some time the usual dress of those in sympathy with the life of sentiment (*Empfindsamkeit*).

51. *p. 94.* The wife of the new vicar is modelled on the Pietest Dorothea Griesbach (1726–75), whom Goethe had met in

Frankfurt at the home of Susanne von Klettenberg (see Note 9). In Book 8 of *Dichtung und Wahrheit* Goethe later referred to Dorothea Griesbach as seeming 'too severe, too dry and too learned'.

52. *p. 94.* The eighteenth century saw the first attempts at textual and historical criticism of the Bible. The English theologian Benjamin Kennicot (1718–83) was pre-eminent in Old Testament textual criticism in Werther's day. Johann Salomo Semler (1725–91) was Professor of Theology at Halle and insisted on the distinction between the Word of God and what was written in the Bible by human hand. Johann David Michaelis (1717–91) laid the foundation, as Professor for Oriental Languages at Göttingen, for undogmatic historical analysis of the Bible.

53. *p. 95.* In 1761–5 an Edinburgh teacher named James Macpherson (1736–96) published a collection of epic fragments purporting to be translations from the Gaelic. A Highlander familiar with Gaelic, he had been encouraged by the revival of interest in the folk tradition to seek out traditional poetry and songs. The fragments he showed to Professor Hugh Blair of the University of Edinburgh were, however, his own work: a gifted blend of motifs, rhythms and attitudes taken from Irish and Scottish folk tales, the Bible, Homer, Milton and more recent nature poetry by a Thomson or a Young. These fragments were supposedly the work of the bard Ossian and told of the deeds of his father Fingal and of other heroes. Professor Blair, enthusiastically certain that a lost epic had been rediscovered, urged publication, and the result was a European bestseller. Herder, who was deeply involved in the revival of the folk tradition, brought the Ossian fragments to Goethe's notice in the winter of 1770–71 in Strassburg, at a time when they were still thought to be genuine. For a taste of Ossian, see pp. 119ff. See also Note 65.

54. *p. 96.* Werther is slightly misquoting a passage from Ossian which he later reads to Lotte. See p. 125.

55. *p. 98*. Compare Ecclesiastes 12:6.

56. *p. 98*. Compare Deuteronomy 28:23.

57. *p. 99*. See John 6:65.

58. *p. 99*. See Matthew 26:39.

59. *p. 99*. Werther is echoing Hamlet's soliloquy at III. i. 56.

60. *p. 100*. See Matthew 27:46.

61. *p. 100*. See Psalms 104:2.

62. *p. 102*. The distracted Heinrich means the Dutch *Staten-Generaal*. The Netherlands were seen as wealthy.

63. *p. 104*. Compare Luke 15:11–24.

64. *p. 113*. Here too Werther is echoing Hamlet. See Note 59.

65. *p. 119*. The passages of Ossian which Werther reads in his own translations were passages from the 'Songs of Selma' which Goethe had himself translated, probably while still in Strassburg. He made a fair copy of them in autumn 1771 as a gift for Friederike Brion. Goethe apparently lost his taste for Ossian fairly rapidly, and the inclusion of Ossian's songs at this point of the novel (when Werther has relinquished Homer in his favour) is intended emblematically. Years later, in 1829, Goethe remarked to Henry Crabb Robinson that 'Werther praised Homer while he retained his senses, and Ossian when he was going mad.' See Note 53.

66. *p. 125*. Goethe based this passage on what he had heard from Kestner concerning Jerusalem's last meeting with Elisabeth Herd.

67. *p. 128*. See John 14:28.

143

68. *p. 128.* This is a slightly less formal version of a note Jerusalem sent to Kestner, dated 29 October 1772. When Goethe was in Wetzlar in November 1772 he took this note into his possession.

69. *p. 132.* After Jerusalem's death it was uncertain whether he would find a resting place in the churchyard, since the Rev. Pilger, a churlish priest of the kind Laertes complained of, opposed the idea. The Count von Spauer, a friend of the deceased, supported the efforts of Heinrich Buff, and Jerusalem was buried in a remote corner of the graveyard; but the Rev. Pilger, according to Friedrich Christian Laukhard, then a student in Giessen, could not forbear from preaching repeated sermons on the evil of suicide.

70. *p. 132.* See Luke 10:31–3.

71. *p. 133.* Compare John 18:11.

72. *p. 134.* A copy of the play *Emilia Galotti* (1772) by Gotthold Ephraim Lessing (1729–81) lay open on Jerusalem's desk when he was found. A middle-class tragedy, the play helped to establish social criticism as a proper concern of the theatre, and perhaps it was this that recommended it to the rejected Jerusalem and the novelist Goethe alike.